THE MODERN READERS' SERIES

ASHLEY H. THORNDIKE, *General Editor*

The Hoosier Schoolmaster

The Hoosier Schoolmaster

A Story of Backwoods Life
in Indiana

By EDWARD EGGLESTON

WITH AN INTRODUCTION BY
EMORY HOLLOWAY
PROFESSOR OF ENGLISH AT ADELPHI COLLEGE

THE MACMILLAN COMPANY

PUBLISHERS   NEW YORK   MCMXXVIII

THE MODERN READERS' SERIES

CONTENTS

		PAGE
Editor's Introduction		vii
Part of the Preface to the First Edition		xxvii

THE HOOSIER SCHOOLMASTER

Chapter I. A Private Lesson from a Bulldog		3
Chapter II. A Spell Coming		15
Chapter III. Mirandy, Hank, and Shocky		19
Chapter IV. Spelling Down the Master		30
Chapter V. The Walk Home		47
Chapter VI. A Night at Pete Jones's		53
Chapter VII. Ominous Remarks of Mr. Jones		60
Chapter VIII. The Struggle in the Dark		63
Chapter IX. Has God Forgotten Shocky?		67
Chapter X. The Devil of Silence		71
Chapter XI. Miss Martha Hawkins		77
Chapter XII. The Hardshell Preacher		84
Chapter XIII. A Struggle for the Mastery		92
Chapter XIV. A Crisis with Bud		98
Chapter XV. The Church of the Best Licks		104
Chapter XVI. The Church Militant		109
Chapter XVII. A Council of War		114
Chapter XVIII. Odds and Ends		119
Chapter XIX. Face to Face		123

Contents

		PAGE
CHAPTER XX. God Remembers Shocky	. . .	127
CHAPTER XXI. Miss Nancy Sawyer	. . .	133
CHAPTER XXII. Pancakes	. . .	135
CHAPTER XXIII. A Charitable Institution	. .	141
CHAPTER XXIV. The Good Samaritan	. . .	148
CHAPTER XXV. Bud Wooing	. . .	151
CHAPTER XXVI. A Letter and its Consequences	. .	155
CHAPTER XXVII. A Loss and a Gain	. . .	158
CHAPTER XXVIII. The Flight	. . .	161
CHAPTER XXIX. The Trial	. . .	166
CHAPTER XXX. "Brother Sodom"	. . .	178
CHAPTER XXXI. The Trial Concluded	. . .	182
CHAPTER XXXII. After the Battle	. . .	194
CHAPTER XXXIII. Into the Light	. . .	198
CHAPTER XXXIV. "How it Came Out"	. . .	201

EDITOR'S INTRODUCTION

INTEREST in Eggleston's most famous novel has probably always been chiefly social and historical rather than strictly literary. Judged by literary standards as established by the type today, it can hardly rank even as his best story. But it would be unfair to estimate it by standards which its own pioneering did so much to introduce. It must be read as a pioneer realistic local-color story. The student of the cultural growth of America will find in it, as nowhere else, a convincing picture of Hoosier life before the Civil War. "This tendency to what the Germans call 'culture-history,'" Eggleston said in summing up his literary career, "is the one distinguishing trait of almost all that I have attempted," whether in fiction or more sober chronicle. Had he lived to complete the ambitious history of the people of the United States—such a book as Green wrote of the English—to which he devoted the arduous scholarship of his last years, he would doubtless have presented the Civil War less as a conflict of moral standards and legal interpretations than as the natural travail of many provincialisms uniting to bring forth a new nation. Such a point of view soon followed the war. When once the emancipation of the slaves and the unequivocal victory of Union arms had rendered obsolete that spirit of assertive superiority wherewith each section had so long justified to itself its distrust of the other, the natural adaptability of a race of pioneers very soon found expression in each section through a great curiosity concerning the life and the people of the other.

"In a kind of astonishment," says Professor Fred Lewis Pattee, "she [America] wandered from section to section of her own land, discovering everywhere peoples and manners and languages that were as strange to her even as foreign lands. Mark Twain and Harte and Miller opened to view the wild regions and wilder society of early California and the Sierra Nevadas; Eggleston pictured the primitive settlements of Indiana; Cable told the romance of the Creoles and of the picturesque descendants of the Acadians on the bayous of Louisiana; Page and Harris and F. H. Smith and others caught a vision of the romance of the old South; Allen told of Kentucky life; Miss French of the dwellers in the canebrakes of Arkansas; and Miss Murfree of a strange people in the Great Smoky Mountains of Tennessee. In twenty years every isolated neighborhood in America had had its chronicler and photographer."

It was therefore not only because of its literary merit but also because of its extreme timeliness that Bret Harte's short story, "The Luck of Roaring Camp," in 1869 set the fashion for local-color studies throughout the whole country. The first popular novel of the type was Eggleston's "The Hoosier Schoolmaster." Harte's stories, however, were the work of an outsider dressing up for romantic effect the more sentimental and melodramatic extravagances of a region without a past. The captivating novelty of "The Hoosier Schoolmaster," on the other hand, lay in its strict fidelity to backwoods life in a section that had been settled long enough to present to the native fictionist a texture of customs, habits and dialect sufficiently rigid for firm and clear treatment. That the first influential realism should have appeared in stories of Indiana was not surprising. "Perhaps some of the barrenness in the life of the Middle West," says Professor Carl Van Doren, "lacking both the longer memories of the Atlantic States and the splendid golden expectations of California, discouraged romance there and set going that tendency towards naturalism which descends unbroken from Edward Eggleston through E.W. Howe and Hamlin Garland, Theodore Dreiser and Edgar Lee Masters." Eggleston was too modest to "suppose that the 'Hoosier Schoolmaster' bore any causative relation to that broader provincial movement," but he did claim that it was "the file-leader of the procession of American dialect novels." The only suggestion American literature offered for the experiment was the example of Lowell in a very different field and form, though Eggleston drew inspiration also from the lesson he got from reading Taine's "Art in the Netherlands," that "the artist of originality will work courageously with the materials he finds in his own environment."

Nor was it wholly accidental that it should have been Eggleston rather than another who was to open this virgin field to letters. The combination of aristocratic Virginia stock with birth and upbringing in the free land north of the Ohio rendered him immune from the sectional astigmatism incompatible with the scientific impersonality of a national realist. While he was of the life he described and had observed it long and intimately, his natural ability, his reading and his travels enabled him to see it objectively. Indeed, he was a little sensitive when an occasional reader was beguiled by the vivid details of his stories into supposing that his stark pictures of Hoosier types were in reality chapters of a disguised autobiography. And yet, speaking of another of the Hoosier stories than the present one, he declared, "Whatever is incredible in this story is true." Bud Means, Shocky, and Jeems Phillips all had their suggestive if not literal prototypes. Eggleston had himself witnessed the trial of Dr. Small's ruffian gang when he was a youthful clerk in a backwoods store—a trial, by the way, whose revelation of the iniquitous hypocrisy of human nature left the impressionable lad ill for a time. "At the age when other children hear fables and fairy stories," he records, "my childish fancy was filled with traditions of battles with Indians and highwaymen. Instead of imaginary giant-killers, children then heard of real Indian-slayers; instead of Blue Beards, we had Murrell and his robbers; instead of Little Red Riding Hood's wolf, we were regaled with the daring adventures of the generation before us with wild beasts on the very road we traveled to school." But to understand how the events and conditions of his personal life equipped him to be the fictional historian of this part of the Middle West, a rapid survey of his biography is essential.

Edward Eggleston was born at Vevay, Indiana, December 10, 1837. This little Ohio River town was the principal one in a county of picturesque natural beauty. To the stimulation which such natural loveliness gave to his youthful fancy he attributed much of his literary ambition. In the great woods near his home he was fond of localizing for his companions the stories of mythology, much as Tom Sawyer employed his miscellaneous reading of adventure stories. Vevay was the political center of Switzerland County, and both names indicate that it was largely settled by the thrifty and virtuous Swiss, whom Eggleston describes sympathetically in "Roxy." There he might study also a considerable number of Germans, Scotch, New Englanders, Kentuckians and a smaller ingredient of the "poor whites" who often serve as the mob villains or border ruffians of his more melodramatic episodes, only to move on to Pike County when overtaken in their villainy. His most intimate contact with this class, however, came when he went to live for a year with a patriarchal uncle in Decatur County.

A man's outlook on life is of course colored by the social environment in which he is born, but still more by the social position with reference to that environment to which he is entitled by birth and training. It was a recognition of this fact that gave Eggleston a certain perspective in his pictures of homely life, and made it possible for him to write of human nature while he was writing of Hoosier manners. As for his own birth, it enabled him to look upon life from the topmost local stratum. His father, Joseph Cary Eggleston, after graduating with highest honors from the law school at William and Mary, had pushed west from the ancestral acres in Virginia and had soon established himself in his profession in Indiana, serving in both houses of the state legislature. He had married an intelligent wife of an equally prominent family, who had likewise come from Virginia, by way of Kentucky. Some of Eggleston's omnivorous bookishness must be traced to a mother who had read "Pilgrim's Progress" through before the age of four. Edward and his brother, George Cary, two years his junior, grew up in an atmosphere of books and intelligent discussion which served as a corrective to the illiteracy, fanatical emotion, and provincialism everywhere about them. The dialect which Eggleston records with such meticulousness was never spoken in his own home.

But from his father, who died of consumption in Edward's tenth year, the latter unfortunately inherited a frail constitution. Throughout his youth he was such a constant sufferer from malaria, winter coughs, and nervous insomnia that he was confidently expected to succumb to his father's fate at an early age. Only once was he able to attend school for as much as three months at a time without a breakdown in health. Indeed, after his tenth year his entire regular schooling amounted to less than eighteen months. But his father, before he died, had provided for his children in two important ways. He instructed his wife to dispose of his law library and to convert the proceeds into books of general literature; and he insisted that the boys should spend every summer working on a farm for their board, that they might grow robust in body and benefit by the training which only manual labor insures.

When, a few years later, Mrs. Eggleston was married a second time, it was to the Rev. Dr. Williamson Terrell, who soon rose to be pastor of the Methodist church at Madison. The removal to a more urban environment doubtless did much to throw into relief in Eggleston's mind the still fresh impressions of his boyhood. And his close contact with a successful Methodist preacher was a determining influence in his decision, a little later, to enter the ministry. The asceticism and austerity of Western Methodism, as Eggleston emphasizes in "The Circuit Rider," were incident to frontier conditions and perhaps essential to its success, but it does not follow that a home life in such an atmosphere was an ideal situation for an intelligent and impressionable boy like himself. "Ill, sensitive, and susceptible," he wrote in detailing the formative influences of his life, "I was tossed like a shuttlecock between two enthusiasms—that for intellectual acquirement, and that for religious devotion . . . Western Methodism was almost as rigorous as Puritanism, and tenfold more ardent. It probably saved me from the vices of village life—more insidious than those of a city—and it gave me a prevailing serious view of life, and stimulated the highest moral aspirations; but it did me harm, also, since the scrupulosity which it bred in one of my temperament impaired my health, and for a time narrowed the range of my intellectual development." The scrupulosity to which he refers caused him at times to go days without uttering more than the most laconic expressions, from fear of incurring the Biblical judgment promised for every idle word. It is reflected in his study of Roxy, of the Presbyterian minister Whittaker, and especially of the circuit riders and of the "faith doctor," Phallida Callendar. And the repression of his intellectual curiosity was manifested in a prolonged refusal to study with his brother the geology of the fossilized rocks about Madison lest such a study undermine his simple faith. He in time became philosopher enough, however, to discover in even such illiberal influences a certain compensation. "Out of the austerity of the middle ages came the renaissance; out of New England Puritanism came the literary productivity of the Unitarian reaction. . . . However misdirected and disproportioned some of the fervid aspirations of my days of religious enthusiasm may have been, I cannot conceive that such experiences were not of use in subsoiling the moral nature. And I also had my period of renaissance—that exhilaration and exultation which the liberated mind feels in the rebound from constraint, and which carries it for a time to a higher level than it might otherwise have attained."

The liberation from such an incubus came slowly, being finally accelerated by such authors as Channing and Emerson; but that it would come sooner or later was insured by the constant development of his mind and character. Though he had little formal education, as has been said, he incessantly taught himself. Acting on the mistaken idea of his day that asceticism and anæmia were conducive to intellectual acuteness and to piety, he would often rouse himself from slumber at four o'clock in the morning to read Xenophon or Virgil. By the time he was twenty-five he had acquaintance with six or seven foreign languages, and had read widely in philosophy, science, *belles lettres*, and religious writings. Association with two persons—who must have been in his mind as he drew the portrait of the Backwoods Philosopher in "The End of the World"—set him on the way toward a saner self-culture. One was Mrs. Julia L. Dumont, a writer of ability, who corrected his compositions with the greater severity because she foresaw that he too would be an author. She was, moreover, a born teacher, who, in a region where the prevailing criterion of pedagogy was "no lickin', no larnin'," selected ten pupils and taught them out of sheer love of teaching. The other liberating influence was his cousin, Guilford Dudley Eggleston. Of him Eggleston says, "He incessantly stimulated my love for literature, guided my choice of books, taught me to make a commonplace book of my reading, and by his conversation and example made me feel that to lead an intellectual life was the most laudable pursuit of a human being."

The predicted breakdown in Edward Eggleston's health came in 1856, when he was eighteen. His mother took him to St. Louis in search of a more congenial climate, and while there he conceived the idea of joining a band of emigrants who were making their way to the territory of Minnesota. Being without funds, he determined to rough it, playing a game in which he knew the stakes to be health or death. Here the training in self-reliance his father's foresight had given him supplied the adaptability he needed. Any employment was worthy of his hand if only it would enable him to survive. He peddled a recipe for soap. He drove three yoke of oxen hitched to a prairie plow. He carried a surveyor's chain, and was soon sufficiently skilled with the transit and compass to command a surveying party himself. And for the first time in his life he was well. But he did not remain in Minnesota very long.

In this year the fierce struggle over free-soil began to rage in Kansas, and Eggleston, with a Methodist's knight-errantry and a frontiersman's willingness to take a hand in a fight, bought the only weapon he could afford, a dirk knife, and set out for Kansas afoot. For he was now an abolitionist, in striking contrast to his brother, who was to distinguish himself in the Southern Army and to write books celebrating the charms of life in the South before the war. At different times both boys had gone to spend a year or more with their numerous relatives in Virginia, but their reactions to slavery were as different as the youths themselves. Edward had not been insensible to the charms and virtues of the *ancien régime*. "The old Virginia country-gentleman life," he once said, "had a fascination not possessed by any other society in the new world. With its unbounded hospitality to all comers, its enormous family pride, its sharp line of distinction between the well-born and the plebeian, its social refinements, its narrow local prejudices, its chivalrous and romantic senti- ment toward ladies, and a certain laxity of morals growing out of the existence of a slave class, could not fail to excite a profound interest in the mind of one who had been bred in a simpler and less dignified society, in which proprieties were less regarded and moralities somewhat more rigidly enforced." And so much was he liked that an uncle offered to adopt him, promising him a coveted education at the University of Virginia and later at some German univer- sity. But Edward's "scrupulosity" forbade him to enjoy the profits of slave labor, and he declined an offer which opened a vista to his fondest dreams. "Though I saw slavery in its mildest form among my relations," he ex- plained, "I could not be blind to its essential and manifold injustices and the unavoidable cruelties of the system. From the time of my visit to Virginia, I counted myself an abolitionist."

The young enthusiast, however, did not reach Kansas.

After weeks of travel his moccasins were worn out, he was footsore, his money was almost gone, he had to limit his rations to crackers and cheese, and he was homesick for civilization after dwelling so long in the rude cabins of the frontier; so that he was not very sorry to find obstacles closing the Kansas boundary on the Iowa side. He decided to go home. "I turned eastward at a point west of Cedar Falls, crossed the Mississippi near Muscatine, and after walking in all three or four hundred miles, I at length boarded a railway train at a little station near Galesburg, and reached my nearest relatives the next morning, after an enforced fast of twenty-four hours, without a cent in my pocket, and looking, in my soiled and travel-worn garments, like a young border ruffian. I had left home a pale invalid; I returned sun-browned and well."

He was not yet nineteen and his desire was still strong to make use of the college scholarship which had been purchased for the boys, but he dared not risk his dearly won health by any employment indoors. So he began to devote his strength to that other ambition, from which he never quite escaped even in his best stories. "Two manner of men were in me, and for the greater part of my life there has been an enduring struggle between the lover of literary art and the religionist, the reformer, the philanthropist, the man with a mission." In that community the possession of any ability in public speech by a pious youth was taken to indicate a fitness for the ministry. Eggleston yielded at once to his own inclination and to the expectation of his family and entered the calling of his step-father. His education being already superior to that of most circuit riders, no objection was raised to his immediate ordination. Packing a little clothing and some books in his saddle-bags, he started out to ride a circuit of ten appointments in the backwoods region of southeastern Indiana.

So zealous was he in his labors to bring the civilizing influences of intelligence and religion to bear upon that wild parish that "at the end of six months," he says, "I was again a candidate for the grave." One perceives by what right of hard experience he could assume to interpret the spirit that actuated the devout and courageous apostles of light in his "tale of the heroic age." Instead of giving up so precarious a calling, however, he rested for a few months and then set off to preach the gospel in Minnesota. "Partly for the sake of my health; more from pure zeal and the desire to be doing the hardest task I could find, I now took up my residence in Minnesota, beginning my labors there by traversing the frontier prairies, on the very border of the Indian country, and in moccasined feet, for I could not afford a horse on the mere promise of a salary, certain never to be half paid." When, later, he did possess a good horse, trouble with the Indians broke out and he joined a company organized to subdue the Indians. With some chagrin he had to turn back, afoot, when his captain kindly intimated to the parson that, being short of horses and long of men, he would rather have a huskier fighter in Eggleston's saddle.

Concerning the preachers with whom he labored, he testified, "It is the privilege of a lifetime to have known a company of men so sincere and disinterested as most of them were." "How do I remember the forms and weather-beaten visages of the old preachers, whose constitutions had conquered starvation and exposure—who had survived swamps, alligators, Indians, highway robbers and bilious fevers!" Perhaps Eggleston did not at the time realize how such a life of self-immolation was preparing in him that imaginative detachment he would need when once his "renaissance" should have made him a fictionist and a scholar. Yet the literary ambition was not dead.

It was not even asleep. From the time he had learned to handle a compositor's stick in order to submit to the Vevay "Reveille" contributions already in type, in the greater hope of their acceptance by a lazy editor, he had never ceased to write. As a preacher most of his contributions were of course sent to denominational papers. It is true that when a certain illiberal-minded elder admonished him, "I question if true consecration is compatible with the literary work you are doing," he burned all his manuscripts. From other motives Hawthorne had done the same; but an Eggleston or a Hawthorne does not so easily escape his destined career. In Indiana Eggleston had bought the slowest horse he could find in order that he might with plausible excuse spend as little time as possible in the dull cabins of his parishioners and as much as possible on the road between appointments, laboriously translating Greek classics, without a lexicon, as he rode. Likewise, in Minnesota, the inner conflict went on. "From the highest motives I risked my life in crossing the prairies afoot, to preach" to Indians, hunters, trappers, white settlers and half-breed voyageurs "in undaubed cabins with the thermometer below zero; but I often carried a volume of poetry, a scientific book, or perhaps a tome of French dramas, to beguile the other man in me."

Having attracted attention by his zeal and ability, he was soon appointed to the largest church in St. Paul. About the same time he married, at the age of twenty. In the Minnesota ministry he remained nine years, but eventually his poor health caused him to turn from preaching to literary work for his livelihood. He had long written children's stories for "The Little Corporal," a successful juvenile publication of Chicago. He now, in 1866, accepted a position as associate editor of the paper, and went to live in Evanston, to be near his work. He collected some of these fanciful, sentimental tales, a few years later, in "A Book of Queer Stories." He also edited the "National Sunday School Teacher," the organ of the rapidly spreading Sunday-school movement. He likewise wrote editorials for a Chicago daily and was general western correspondent for the then influential New York "Independent," edited by Theodore Tilton. His work for "The Independent" was so well received that within a year he was asked to join the staff of the magazine. He did so, and moved his residence to Brooklyn. When, shortly afterwards, Tilton severed his connection with the periodical, Eggleston took his desk. But within seven months he too left "The Independent" because of his conscientious objection to the political policy of the paper. In this short time, however, he had made acquaintance with most of the promising and established writers of the country.

This contact with the best authors made it possible for him to resuscitate the "Hearth and Home," when he was almost immediately called to take charge of that illustrated weekly. Under the inexperienced editing of Harriet Beecher Stowe and Donald Grant Mitchell, it was all but defunct. Eggleston's brother, who by this time had given up the practice of law for journalism, was installed as business manager, Frank R. Stockton was added to the staff, and authors like Edward Everett Hale, John Esten Cooke, E. P. Roe, Louisa M. Alcott, Rebecca Harding Davis, Harriet Prescott Spofford, and Helen Hunt were induced to contribute. But the chief cause of the sudden multiplication of subscribers was the serial publication of "The Hoosier Schoolmaster." One of Eggleston's innovations was the running of short stories in the "Hearth and Home," and it was his original intention merely to contribute a three-number story based, in part, on his brother's early experiences as a school-teacher at Riker's Ridge.

But the widespread interest immediately awakened by the story persuaded him, after the first installment, to enlarge the narrative to the size of a small book. This meant that he had to run a race with the printer in writing the story, a fact which, taken with his imperfect knowledge of novel technique and his limited acquaintance with possible models, accounts largely for the crude and amateurish construction of the plot. Of Hoosier manners, however, the main thing, he could write without much deliberation. In fact, during the war he had published a story in Indiana dialect in a St. Paul paper, and he had projected a lecture on the Hoosier folk speech.

The serial publication completed, the story was issued as an unattractive-looking book (1872), with the original illustrations and in the original newspaper type. Yet it proved to be the best-selling book of fiction in its day. Fifty thousand copies were sold in a few months and for a generation the sales averaged over two thousand a year. Translations were published in Dutch, Danish, French, and German. Such unprecedented success in his experiment naturally led the editor of "Hearth and Home" to dig again in the Hoosier mine. The result was "The End of the World," a story whose plot would be frail indeed but for the introduction of the Millerite excitement which Eggleston had observed in 1842–43. It contains, however, two authentic, if hastily drawn, characters and shows that, before Mark Twain, Eggleston had found the river steamboat useful in a western romance. For all its faults, the serial did not retard the growing circulation of the newspaper, but induced its publishers to relieve Eggleston from all his editorial duties that he might write still another serial, "The Mystery of Metropolisville." The title of this story is somewhat misleading, for the "mystery" appears only in the last third of the book. The background here is Minnesota, at the time of its first railway development; and what interest the story may hold lies in the author's characterization of boom towns and their makers. It is interesting to note, what seems not to have been observed before, that it was while Eggleston's story was running in "Hearth and Home" (December, 1872–April, 1873) that an after-dinner discussion concerning what fiction should be led Mark Twain and Charles Dudley Warner to plan and to write in collaboration "The Gilded Age" (finished in April, 1873), which makes such large use of similar material. Mark Twain had first-hand sources of information, it is true, and is said to have long considered making fictional use of them; but to Eggleston's story belongs the credit of prior publication, if not that of having provoked the more readable, if equally melodramatic, story of Twain and Warner.

With his third story Eggleston did well to be dissatisfied. The author wrote too rapidly, relied too largely on memory instead of on inventive imagination, and drew scarcely a single consistent or impressive character. He may have driven his plowshare, as the "Hearth and Home" asserted, into a richer field than that in which he had made his reputation, but the materials were refractory, at least for any but a great artist, which Eggleston was not. As his brother said, "There were no well-defined characteristics, no prevalent habits, customs or ideas that the novelist could seize upon." The author's plan to write no more novels until he could write better ones, however, was not immediately to be carried out. Fortunately he yielded to persuasion and agreed to write for "The Christian Union" a story called "The Circuit Rider: A Tale of the Heroic Age." In it he returns to the Hoosier backgrounds though the scene is laid in southern Illinois. In several of his other stories Eggleston had introduced Methodist ministers, but usually he had so foiled their physical courage and illiterate zeal against the more highly educated and decorous representatives of other faiths as to produce an effect not unlike caricature. The illustrations in the books did nothing to soften this effect. But in "The Circuit Rider" one feels that the objective realist is for once writing out of his own experience. The result is a dignity and directness that befits his epic theme. The inevitable melodrama is of the time. The characters are carefully foiled to bring out the personal elements in a highly personal religion, and to present to the reader a type of hero which is as extinct as Natty Bumppo. Thus, writing of a high theme with sympathetic comprehension, he has given to American Methodism its one classic story. Eggleston's growing liberalism of thought, though it finally destroyed his faith in the supernatural entirely, never led him to qualify his admiration for these spiritual heroes whose unenlightened minds could not dim their glowing hearts.

In 1874 Eggleston accepted his last charge as a minister. But it was not now as a Methodist; indeed, it was not as spokesman for any denomination. He agreed to serve as pastor of the Lee Congregational Church of Brooklyn only on condition that no creed should be emphasized, the only qualification expected of members being a desire to serve others. Accordingly the church was rechristened "The Church of Christian Endeavor," a name reminiscent of Bud Mean's Church of the Best Licks, and also adopted by a young people's religious organization of national scope. The church prospered under Eggleston's ministry; but after four years he was compelled to resign because of failing health. This he blamed chiefly on that lifelong scrupulosity, which kept him in constant dread lest any sort of ministerial work might seem to commit him to doctrines that he did not hold. The remainder of his life, twenty-two years, was spent in study and writing. First he went abroad in search of health—to Switzerland, to Italy, to France and England. He spent much time in the libraries of Europe collecting historical material for his *magnum opus*, never to be finished. These studies were continued when he returned to America, especially at his retreat at Lake George. It was at his Lake George home that he died, in 1902, from apoplexy.

During these last years, however, Eggleston did most of his best writing. Before leaving Brooklyn he had published "Roxy," certainly among the best of his Hoosier stories. As in the case of his earlier stories, the main plot is based on an actual occurrence, this time the heroine being a wife who forgives both her erring husband and his paramour; but into the background Eggleston has introduced enough carefully drawn characters and customs to give the story life. The hard-cider campaign, the backwoods politician, the circuit rider, the school-teacher, the village gossip, the rustic amusements, the Swiss interiors, the Methodist revivals,—all are woven into a closely knit narrative, which the author has presented with the sympathy and understanding of a mature mind. While at Venice he wrote "The Hoosier Schoolboy," a belated companion-piece to "The Hoosier Schoolmaster." It is a slender but creditable genre study, limiting itself to the schoolboy's point of view; but, perhaps for the reason that Eggleston had never been a typical schoolboy himself, he fails to get as much out of his material as Mark Twain did with similar opportunities. A better story, written about the same time, was "The Graysons." Again he digs in his special mine, presenting the Hoosier life of the younger generation. The backgrounds are often skimped in this story, but the characters are real, and the action culminates in a thrilling court-room scene in which Abraham Lincoln, according to the legend, serves as a legal *deus ex machina*. Only two volumes were completed of "A History of the United States and Its People," which sought to do for the whole country a service of social interpretation similar to that which the author's stories had done for the Hoosiers. One more novel he was to compose, "The Faith Doctor." The idea of the story was borrowed, though only the idea, and that with due acknowledgment; but the occasion was Eggleston's desire to attack the "prevailing interest in mind-cure, faith-cure, Christian science and other sorts of aërial therapeutics." Remembering the preacher-artist he confessed himself to be, one cannot quite allow his claim that his purpose was artistic rather than polemical. But if the book be weakened a little by its left-handed defense of his own thorough-going rationalism, it has, as George Cary Eggleston points out, an element of enlightening autobiography in its analysis of that "lust for perfection" which tortured Eggleston's own youth. "Duffels," published in 1893, is probably the best collection of Eggleston's short stories, but in this exacting form of fiction, it must be said, Eggleston did not distinguish himself.

As to the place of "The Hoosier Schoolmaster" in American literary history, little remains to be noted. In his preface to the library edition published twenty years after its first appearance, Eggleston frankly admits, "No one knows so well as I the faults of immaturity and inexperience that characterize this book." He had passed so far beyond it in narrative skill and in maturity of thought and sentiment that he no longer felt himself the author of the story. What those faults are the most inexperienced reader can easily name. The plot is melodramatic, and, though based on fact, has the weakness of melodrama. The characters are, almost without exception, mere types, wanting vitality enough to outlive the last chapter. Take from them their once novel dialect, which is not always consistent, and they stand revealed as the creations of a very youthful imagination. The footnotes in the revised edition, originally intended for the first, betray the fact that the author's interest lay more in an experimental study of social conditions than in telling a story for its own sake. The humor, forced and at times facetious in its needless repetition, no less than the illustrative caricatures wherewith a second-rate artist flattered the urban readers of "Hearth and Home," weakens the effect of the book even as a piece of realism. And finally, the influence of Eggleston's previous writing, almost all of it addressed to juveniles, appears in a form of sententiousness and sentimentality he could hardly have learned even from Dickens, though he did once imitate "The Christmas Carol."

And yet the significance of the book as the "file-leader of American dialect novels" and as a social and historical document increases with every year that separates the reader from the age it describes. There may be nothing very penetrating in its insight into human nature or human conditions, but it is a carefully detailed report, as far as it goes, and is not without a certain culminating interest as a story. There is an artlessness in its description which gives it a permanent place among the genre studies of a new land. And its success not only inspired Eggleston to a literary life without which American literature would be poorer, but it encouraged writers in every part of the country to compare notes of their local conditions with his.   EMORY HOLLOWAY

PART OF THE PREFACE TO THE
FIRST EDITION

I MAY as well confess, what it would be affectation to conceal, that I am more than pleased with the generous reception accorded to this story as a serial in the columns of *Hearth and Home*. It has been in my mind since I was a Hoosier boy to do something toward describing life in the back-country districts of the Western States. It used to be a matter of no little jealousy with us, I remember, that the manners, customs, thoughts, and feelings of New England country people filled so large a place in books, while our life, not less interesting, not less romantic, and certainly not less filled with humorous and grotesque material, had no place in literature. It was as though we were shut out of good society. And, with the single exception of Alice Cary, perhaps, our Western writers did not dare speak of the West otherwise than as the unreal world to which Cooper's lively imagination had given birth.

I had some anxiety lest Western readers should take offence at my selecting what must always seem an exceptional phase of life to those who have grown up in the more refined regions of the West. But nowhere has the School-master been received more kindly than in his own country and among his own people.

Some of those who have spoken generous words of the School-master and his friends have suggested that the story is an autobiography. But it is not, save in the sense in which every work of art is an autobiography: in that it is the result of the experience and observation of the writer.

Readers will therefore bear in mind that not Ralph nor Bud nor Brother Sodom nor Dr. Small represents the writer, nor do I appear, as Talleyrand said of Madame de Staël, "disguised as a woman," in the person of Hannah or Mirandy. Some of the incidents have been drawn from life; none of them, I believe, from my own. I should like to be considered a member of the Church of the Best Licks, however.

It has been in my mind to append some remarks, philological and otherwise, upon the dialect, but Professor Lowell's admirable and erudite preface to the Biglow Papers must be the despair of every one who aspires to write on Americanisms. To Mr. Lowell belongs the distinction of being the only one of our most eminent authors and the only one of our most eminent scholars who has given careful attention to American dialects. But while I have not ventured to discuss the provincialisms of the Indiana backwoods, I have been careful to preserve the true *usus loquendi* of each locution.

BROOKLYN, DECEMBER 1871.

THE HOOSIER SCHOOLMASTER

AS A PEBBLE CAST UPON A GREAT CAIRN, THIS EDITION IS INSCRIBED TO THE MEMORY OF JAMES RUSSELL LOWELL, WHOSE CORDIAL ENCOURAGEMENT TO MY EARLY STUDIES OF AMERICAN DIALECT IS GRATEFULLY REMEMBERED.

THE AUTHOR.

THE HOOSIER SCHOOLMASTER

CHAPTER I

A PRIVATE LESSON FROM A BULLDOG

"WANT to be a schoolmaster, do you? You? Well, what would *you* do in Flat Crick deestrick, *I'd* like to know? Why, the boys have driv off the last two, and licked the one afore them like blazes. You might teach a summer school, when nothin' but children come. But I 'low it takes a right smart *man* to be schoolmaster in Flat Crick in the winter. They'd pitch you out of doors, sonny, neck and heels, afore Christmas."

The young man, who had walked ten miles to get the school in this district, and who had been mentally reviewing his learning at every step he took, trembling lest the committee should find that he did not know enough, was not a little taken aback at this greeting from "old Jack Means," who was the first trustee that he lighted on. The impression made by these ominous remarks was emphasized by the glances which he received from Jack Means's two sons. The older one eyed him from the top of his brawny shoulders with that amiable look which a big dog turns on a little one before shaking him. Ralph Hartsook had never thought of being

3

measured by the standard of muscle. This notion of beating education into young savages in spite of themselves dashed his ardor.

He had walked right to where Jack Means was at work shaving shingles in his own front yard. While Mr. Means was making the speech which we have set down above, and punctuating it with expectorations, a large brindle bulldog had been sniffing at Ralph's heels, and a girl in a new linsey-woolsey dress, standing by the door, had nearly giggled her head off at the delightful prospect of seeing a new school-teacher eaten up by the ferocious brute.

The disheartening words of the old man, the immense muscles of the young man who was to be his rebellious pupil, the jaws of the ugly bulldog, and the heartless giggle of the girl, gave Ralph a delightful sense of having precipitated himself into a den of wild beasts. Faint with weariness and discouragement, and shivering with fear, he sat down on a wheelbarrow.

"You, Bull!" said the old man to the dog, which was showing more and more a disposition to make a meal of the incipient pedagogue, "you, Bull! git aout,[1] you pup!" The dog walked sullenly off, but not until he had given Ralph a look full of promise of what he meant to do when he got a good chance. Ralph wished himself back in the village of Lewisburg, whence he had come.

"You see," continued Mr. Means, spitting in a

---

[1] *Aout* is not the common form of *out*, as it is in certain rustic New England regions. The vowel is here drawn in this way for imperative emphasis, and it occurs as a consequence of drawling speech.

meditative sort of a way, "you see, we a'n't none of your saft sort in these diggin's. It takes a *man* to boss this deestrick. Howsumdever, ef you think you kin trust your hide in Flat Crick schoolhouse I ha'n't got no 'bjection. But ef you git licked, don't come on us. Flat Crick don't pay no 'nsurance, you bet! Any other trustees? Wal, yes. But as I pay the most taxes, t'others jist let me run the thing. You can begin right off a Monday. They a'n't been no other applications. You see, it takes grit to apply for this school. The last master had a black eye for a month. But, as I wuz sayin', you can jist roll up and wade in. I 'low you've got spunk, maybe, and that goes for a heap sight more'n sinnoo with boys. Walk in, and stay over Sunday with me. You'll hev' to board roun', and I guess you better begin here."

Ralph did not go in, but sat out on the wheelbarrow, watching the old man shave shingles, while the boys split the blocks and chopped wood. Bull smelled of the new-comer again in an ugly way, and got a good kick from the older son for his pains. But out of one of his red eyes the dog warned the young schoolmaster that *he* should yet suffer for all kicks received on his account.

"Ef Bull once takes a holt, heaven and yarth can't make him let go," said the older son to Ralph, by way of comfort.

It was well for Ralph that he began to "board roun'" by stopping at Mr. Means's. Ralph felt that Flat Creek was what he needed. He had lived a bookish life; but here was his lesson in the art of managing people, for he who can manage the untamed and strapping youths of a winter school in Hoopole County has gone far toward learning one of the hardest of lessons. And in Ralph's time, things were worse than they are now. The older son of Mr. Means was called Bud Means. What his real name was, Ralph could not find out, for in many of these families the nickname of "Bud" given to the oldest boy, and that of "Sis," which is the birthright of the oldest girl, completely bury the proper Christian name. Ralph saw his first strategic point, which was to capture Bud Means.

After supper, the boys began to get ready for something. Bull stuck up his ears in a dignified way, and the three or four yellow curs who were Bull's satellites yelped delightedly and discordantly.

"Bill," said Bud Means to his brother, "ax the master ef he'd like to hunt coons. I'd like to take the starch out uv the stuck-up feller."

"'Nough said,"[1] was Bill's reply.

"You durn't[2] do it," said Bud.

"I don't take no sech a dare,"[3] returned Bill, and walked down to the gate, by which Ralph stood

---

[1] "'Nough said" is more than enough said for the French translator, who takes it apparently for a sort of barbarous negative and renders it, "I don't like to speak to him." I need hardly explain to any American reader that *enough said* implies the ending of all discussion by the acceptance of the proposition or challenge.

[2] *Durn't, daren't, dasent, dursent,* and *don't dast* are forms of this variable negative heard in the folk-speech of various parts of the country. The tenses of this verb seem to have got hopelessly mixed long ago, even in literary use, and the speech of the people reflects the historic confusion.

[3] *To take a dare* is an expression used in senses diametrically opposed. Its common sense is that of the text. The man who refuses to accept a challenge is said to take a dare, and there is some implication of cowardice in the imputation. On the other hand, one who accepts a challenge is said also to take the dare.

watching the stars come out, and half wishing he
had never seen Flat Creek.

"I say, mister," began Bill, "mister, they's a coon
what's been a eatin' our chickens lately, and we're
goin' to try to ketch[1] the varmint. You wouldn't
like to take a coon hunt nor nothin', would you?"

"Why, yes," said Ralph, "there's nothing I should
like better, if I could only be sure Bull wouldn't
mistake me for the coon."

And so, as a matter of policy, Ralph dragged his
tired legs eight or ten miles, on hill and in hollow,
after Bud, and Bill, and Bull, and the coon. But
the raccoon[2] climbed a tree. The boys got into a
quarrel about whose business it was to have brought
the axe, and who was to blame that the tree could
not be felled. Now, if there was anything Ralph's
muscles were good for, it was climbing. So, asking
Bud to give him a start, he soon reached the limb
above the one on which the raccoon was. Ralph
did not know how ugly a customer a raccoon can
be, and so got credit for more courage than he had.
With much peril to his legs from the raccoon's teeth,
he succeeded in shaking the poor creature off among

---

[1] Most bad English was once good English. *Ketch* was used by writers of the
sixteenth and seventeenth centuries for *catch*. A New Hampshire magistrate in
the seventeenth century spells it *caitch*, and probably pronounced it in that way.
Ketch, a boat, was sometimes spelled *catch* by the first American colonists, and
the far-fetched derivation of the word from the Turkish may be one of the fancies
of etymologists.

[2] The derivation of *raccoon* from the French *raton*, to which Mr. Skeat gives
currency, still holds its place in some of our standard dictionaries. If American
lexicographers would only read the literature of American settlement they would
know that Mr. Skeat's citation of a translation of Buffon is nearly two centuries
too late. As early as 1612 Captain John Smith gives *aroughcume* as the aborig-
inal Virginia word, and more than one New England writer used *rackoon* a few
years later.

the yelping brutes and yelling boys. Ralph could not help sympathizing with the hunted animal, which sold its life as dearly as possible, giving the dogs many a scratch and bite. It seemed to him that he was like the raccoon, precipitated into the midst of a party of dogs who would rejoice in worrying *his* life out, as Bull and his crowd were destroying the poor raccoon. When Bull at last seized the raccoon and put an end to it, Ralph could not but admire the decided way in which he did it, calling to mind Bud's comment, "Ef Bull once takes a holt, heaven and yarth[1] can't make him let go."

But as they walked home, Bud carrying the raccoon by the tail, Ralph felt that his hunt had not been in vain. He fancied that even red-eyed Bull, walking uncomfortably close to his heels, respected him more since he had climbed that tree.

"Purty peart kind of a master," remarked the old man to Bud, after Ralph had gone to bed. "Guess you better be a little easy on him. Hey?"

But Bud deigned no reply. Perhaps because he knew that Ralph heard the conversation through the thin partition.

Ralph woke delighted to find it raining. He did not want to hunt or fish on Sunday, and this steady

---

[1] This prefixed *y* is a mark of a very illiterate or antique form of the dialect. I have known *piece yarthen* used for "a piece of earthen"[ware], the preposition getting lost in the sound of the *y*. I leave it to etymologists to determine its relation to that ancient prefix that differentiates *earn* in one sense from *yearn*. But the article before a vowel may account for it if we consider it a corruption. "The earth" pronounced in a drawling way will produce *the yearth*. In the New York Documents is a letter from one Barnard Hodges, a settler in Delaware in the days of Governor Andros, whose spelling indicates a free use of the parasitic *y*. He writes "yunless," "yeunder" (under), "yunderstanding," "yeundertake," and "yeouffeis" (office).

rain would enable him to make friends with Bud. I do not know how he got started, but after breakfast he began to tell stories. Out of all the books he had ever read he told story after story. And "old man Means," and "old *Miss* Means," and Bud Means, and Bill Means, and Sis Means listened with great eyes while he told of Sinbad's adventures, of the Old Man of the Sea, of Robinson Crusoe, of Captain Gulliver's experiences in Liliput, and of Baron Munchausen's exploits.

Ralph had caught his fish. The hungry minds of these backwoods people were refreshed with the new life that came to their imaginations in these stories. For there was but one book in the Means library, and that, a well-thumbed copy of "Captain Riley's Narrative," had long since lost all freshness.

"I'll be dog-on'd,"[1] said Bill, emphatically, "ef I

---

[1] Like many of the ear-marks of this dialect, the verb "dog-on" came from Scotland, presumably by the way of the north of Ireland. A correspondent of *The Nation* calls attention to the use of "dagon" as Scotch dialect in Barrie's "Little Minister," a recent book. On examining that story, I find that the word has precisely the sense of our Hoosier "dog-on," which is to be pronounced broadly as a Hoosier pronounces dog—"daug-on." If Mr. Barrie gives his *a* the broad sound, his "dagon" is nearly identical with "dog-on." Here are some detached sentences from "The Little Minister:"

"Beattie spoke for more than himself when he said: 'Dagon that Manse! I never gie a swear but there it is glowering at me.'"

"'Dagon religion,' Rob retorted fiercely; ''t spoils a' thing.'"

"There was some angry muttering from the crowd, and young Charles Yuill exclaimed, 'Dagon you, would you lord it ower us on week-days as well as on Sabbaths?'"

"'Have you on your Sabbath shoon or have you no on your Sabbath shoon?' 'Guid care you took I should ha'e the dagont things on!' retorted the farmer."

It will be seen that "dagont," as used above, is the Scotch form of "dog-oned." But Mr. Barrie uses the same form apparently for "dog-on it" in the following passage:

"Ay, there was Ruth when she was na wanted, but Ezra, dagont-it looked as if Ezra had jumped clean out o' the Bible!"

hadn't 'ruther hear the master tell them whoppin'
yarns than to go to a circus the best day I ever seed!"
Bill could pay no higher compliment.

What Ralph wanted was to make a friend of Bud.
It's a nice thing to have the seventy-four-gun ship
on your own side, and the more Hartsook admired
the knotted muscles of Bud Means the more he desired to attach him to himself. So, whenever he
struck out a peculiarly brilliant passage, he anxiously
watched Bud's eye. But the young Philistine kept
his own counsel. He listened, but said nothing, and
the eyes under his shaggy brows gave no sign. Ralph
could not tell whether those eyes were deep and
inscrutable or only stolid. Perhaps a little of both.
When Monday morning came, Ralph was nervous.
He walked to school with Bud.

Strangely enough, this word as a verb is not to be found in Jamieson's dictionary of the Scottish dialect, but Jamieson gives "dugon" as a noun. It is
given in the supplement to Jamieson, however, as "dogon," but still as a noun,
with an ancient plural *dogonis*. It is explained as "a term of contempt." The
example cited by Jamieson is Hogg's "Winter Tales," 1. 292, and is as follows:

"What wad my father say if I were to marry a man that loot himsel' be thrashed
by Tommy Potts, a great supple wi' a back nae stiffer than a willy brand? . . .
When one comes to close quarters wi' him he's but a dugon."

Halliwell and Wright give *dogon* as a noun, and mark it Anglo-Norman, but
they apparently know it only from Jamieson and the supplement to Jamieson,
where *dogguin* is cited from Cotgrave as meaning "a filthie old curre," and *doguin*
from Roquefort, defined by "brutal, currish" [hargneux]. A word with the same
orthography, *doguin*, is still used in French for puppy. It is of course a question
whether the noun *dogon* and its French antecedents are connected with the
American verb *dog-on*. It is easy to conceive that such an epithet as *dogon* might
get itself mixed up with the word dog, and so become an imprecation. For
instance, a servant in the family of a friend of mine in Indiana, wishing to
resign her place before the return of some daughters of the house whom she had
never seen, announced that she was going to leave "before them dog-on girls got
home." Here the word might have been the old epithet, or an abbreviated
participle. *Dogged* is apparently a corruption of dog-on in the phrase "I'll be
dogged." I prefer *dog-on* to *dogone*, because in the dialect the sense of setting a
dog on is frequently present to the speaker, though far enough away from the
primitive sense of the word, perhaps.

"I guess you're a little skeered by what the old man said, a'n't you?"

Ralph was about to deny it, but on reflection concluded that it was best to speak the truth. He said that Mr. Means's description of the school had made him feel a little down-hearted.

"What will you do with the tough boys? You a'n't no match for 'em." And Ralph felt Bud's eyes not only measuring his muscles, but scrutinizing his countenance. He only answered:

"I don't know."

"What would you do with me, for instance?" and Bud stretched himself up as if to shake out the reserve power coiled up in his great muscles.

"I sha'n't have any trouble with you."

"Why, I'm the wust chap of all. I thrashed the last master, myself."

And again the eyes of Bud Means looked out sharply from his shadowing brows to see the effect of this speech on the slender young man.

"You won't thrash me, though," said Ralph.

"Pshaw! I 'low I could whip you in an inch of your life with my left hand, and never half try," said young Means, with a threatening sneer.

"I know that as well as you do."

"Well, a'n't you afraid of me, then?" and again he looked sidewise at Ralph.

"Not a bit," said Ralph, wondering at his own courage.

They walked on in silence a minute. Bud was turning the matter over.

"Why a'n't you afraid of me?" he said presently.

"Because you and I are going to be friends."

"And what about t'others?"

"I am not afraid of all the other boys put together."

"You a'n't! The mischief! How's that?"

"Well, I'm not afraid of them because you and I are going to be friends, and you can whip all of them together. You'll do the fighting and I'll do the teaching."

The diplomatic Bud only chuckled a little at this; whether he assented to the alliance or not Ralph could not tell.

When Ralph looked round on the faces of the scholars—the little faces full of mischief and curiosity, the big faces full of an expression which was not further removed than second-cousin from contempt —when young Hartsook looked into these faces, his heart palpitated with stage-fright. There is no audience so hard to face as one of school-children, as many a man has found to his cost. Perhaps it is that no conventional restraint can keep down their laughter when you do or say anything ridiculous.

Hartsook's first day was hurried and unsatisfactory. He was not master of himself, and consequently not master of anybody else. When evening came, there were symptoms of insubordination through the whole school. Poor Ralph was sick at heart. He felt that if there had ever been the shadow of an alliance between himself and Bud, it was all "off" now. It seemed to Hartsook that even Bull had lost his respect for the teacher. Half that night the young man lay awake. At last comfort came to him. A reminiscence of the death of the raccoon flashed on him like a vision. He remembered that quiet and annihilating bite which Bull gave. He remembered Bud's certificate, that "Ef Bull once takes a holt, heaven and yarth can't make him let go." He thought that what Flat Creek needed was a bulldog. He would be a bull-dog, quiet, but invincible. He would take hold in such a way that nothing should make him let go. And then he went to sleep.

In the morning Ralph got out of bed slowly. He put his clothes on slowly. He pulled on his boots in a bulldog mood. He tried to move as he thought Bull would move if he were a man. He ate with deliberation, and looked everybody in the eyes with a manner that made Bud watch him curiously. He found himself continually comparing himself with Bull. He found Bull possessing a strange fascina-tion for him. He walked to school alone, the rest having gone on before. He entered the schoolroom preserving a cool and dogged manner. He saw in the eyes of the boys that there was mischief brewing. He did not dare sit down in his chair for fear of a pin. Everybody looked solemn. Ralph lifted the lid of his desk. "Bow-wow! wow-wow!" It was the voice of an imprisoned puppy, and the school giggled and then roared. Then everything was quiet.

The scholars expected an outburst of wrath from the teacher. For they had come to regard the whole world as divided into two classes, the teacher on the one side representing lawful authority, and the pupils on the other in a state of chronic rebellion.

To play a trick on the master was an evidence of spirit; to "lick" the master was to be the crowned hero of Flat Creek district. Such a hero was Bud Means; and Bill, who had less muscle, saw a chance to distinguish himself on a teacher of slender frame. Hence the puppy in the desk.

Ralph Hartsook grew red in the face when he saw the puppy. But the cool, repressed, bulldog mood in which he had kept himself saved him. He lifted the dog into his arms and stroked him until the laughter subsided. Then, in a solemn and set way, he began:

"I am sorry," and he looked round the room with a steady, hard eye—everybody felt that there was a conflict coming—"I am sorry that any scholar in this school could be so mean"—the word was uttered with a sharp emphasis, and all the big boys felt sure that there would be a fight with Bill Means, and perhaps with Bud—"could be so *mean*—as to —shut up his *brother* in such a place as that!"

There was a long, derisive laugh. The wit was indifferent, but by one stroke Ralph had carried the whole school to his side. By the significant glances of the boys, Hartsook detected the perpetrator of the joke, and with the hard and dogged look in his eyes, with just such a look as Bull would give a puppy, but with the utmost suavity in his voice, he said:

"William Means, will you be so good as to put this dog out of doors?"

CHAPTER II

A SPELL COMING

THERE was a moment of utter stillness; but the magnetism of Ralph's eye was too much for Bill Means. The request was so polite, the master's look was so innocent and yet so determined. Bill often wondered afterward that he had not "fit" rather than obeyed the request. But somehow he put the dog out. He was partly surprised, partly inveigled, partly awed into doing just what he had not intended to do. In the week that followed, Bill had to fight half a dozen boys for calling him "Puppy Means." Bill said he wished he'd licked the master on the spot. 'Twould 'a' saved five fights out of the six.

And all that day and the next, the bulldog in the master's eye was a terror to evil-doers. At the close of school on the second day Bud was heard to give it as his opinion that "the master wouldn't be much in a tussle, but he had a heap of thunder and lightning in him."

Did he inflict corporal punishment? inquires some philanthropic friend. Would you inflict corporal punishment if you were tiger-trainer in Van Amburgh's happy family? But poor Ralph could never satisfy his constituency in this regard.

"Don't believe he'll do," was Mr. Pete Jones's

comment to Mr. Means. "Don't thrash enough. Boys won't l'arn 'less you thrash 'em, says I. Leastways, mine won't. Lay it on good is what I says to a master. Lay it on good. Don't do no harm. Lickin' and l'arnin' goes together. No lickin', no l'arnin', says I. Lickin' and l'arnin', lickin' and larnin', is the good ole way."

And Mr. Jones, like some wiser people, was the more pleased with his formula that it had an alliterative sound. Nevertheless, Ralph was master from this time until the spelling-school came. If only it had not been for that spelling-school! Many and many a time after the night of the fatal spelling-school Ralph used to say, "If only it had not been for that spelling-school!"

There had to be a spelling-school. Not only for the sake of my story, which would not have been worth the telling if the spelling-school had not taken place, but because Flat Creek district had to have a spelling-school. It is the only public literary exercise known in Hoopole County. It takes the place of lyceum lecture and debating club. Sis Means, or, as she wished now to be called, Mirandy Means, expressed herself most positively in favor of it. She said that she 'lowed the folks in that district couldn't in no wise do without it. But it was rather to its social than to its intellectual benefits that she referred. For all the spelling-schools ever seen could not enable her to stand anywhere but at the foot of the class. There is one branch diligently taught in a backwoods school. The public mind seems impressed with the difficulties of English orthography, and there is a solemn conviction that the chief end of man is to learn to spell. " 'Know Webster's Elementary' came down from Heaven," would be the backwoods version of the Greek saying but that, unfortunately for the Greeks, their fame has not reached so far. It often happens that the pupil does not know the meaning of a single word in the lesson. This is of no consequence. What do you want to know the meaning of a word for? Words were made to be spelled, and men were probably created that they might spell them. Hence the necessity for sending a pupil through the spelling-book five times before you allow him to begin to read, or indeed to do anything else. Hence the necessity for those long spelling-classes at the close of each forenoon and afternoon session of the school, to stand at the head of which is the cherished ambition of every scholar. Hence, too, the necessity for devoting the whole of the afternoon session of each Friday to a "spelling-match." In fact, spelling is the "national game" in Hoopole County. Baseball and croquet matches are as unknown as Olympian chariot-races. Spelling and shucking[1] are the only public competitions.

---

[1] In naming the several parts of the Indian corn and the dishes made from it, the English language was put to many shifts. Such words as *tassel* and *silk* were poetically applied to the blossoms; *stalk*, *blade*, and *ear* were borrowed from other sorts of corn, and the Indian tongues were forced to pay tribute to name the dishes borrowed from the savages. From them we have *hominy*, *pone*, *supawn*, and *succotash*. For other nouns words were borrowed from English provincial dialects. *Shuck* is one of these. On the northern belt, shucks are the outer covering of nuts; in the middle and southern regions the word is applied to what in New England is called the husks of the corn. *Shuck*, however, is much more widely used than *husk* in colloquial speech—the farmers in more than half of the United States are hardly acquainted with the word *husk* as applied to the envelope of the ear. *Husk*, in the Middle States, and in some parts of the South and West, means the bran of the cornmeal, as notably in Davy Crockett's verse:

So the fatal spelling-school had to be appointed for the Wednesday of the second week of the session, just when Ralph felt himself master of the situation. Not that he was without his annoyances. One of Ralph's troubles in the week before the spelling-school was that he was loved. The other that he was hated. And while the time between the appointing of the spelling tournament and the actual occurrence of that remarkable event is engaged in elapsing, let me narrate two incidents that made it for Ralph a trying time.

> "She sifted the meat, she gimme the hus';
> She baked the bread, she gimme the crus';
> She b'iled the meat, she gimme the bone;
> She gimme a kick and sent me home."

In parts of Virginia, before the war, the word *husk* or *hus'* meant the cob or spike of the corn. "I smack you over wid a cawn-hus'" is a threat I have often heard one negro boy make to another. *Cob* is provincial English for ear, and I have known "a cob of corn" used in Canada for an ear of Indian corn. While writing this note "a cob of Indian corn"—meaning an ear—appears in the report of an address by a distinguished man at a recent meeting of the Royal Geographical Society. A lady tells me that she met, in the book of an English traveller, the remarkable statement that "the Americans are very fond of the young grain called cob." These Indian-corn words have reached an accepted meaning after a competition. To *shell* corn, among the earliest settlers of Virginia, meant to take it out of the envelope, which was presumably called the shell. The analogy is with the shelling of pulse.

CHAPTER III

Mirandy had nothing but contempt for the new master until he developed the bulldog in his character. Mirandy fell in love with the bulldog. Like many other girls of her class, she was greatly enamored with the "subjection of women," and she stood ready to fall in love with any man strong enough to be her master. Much has been said of the strong-minded woman. I offer this psychological remark as a contribution to the natural history of the weak-minded woman.

It was at the close of that very second day on which Ralph had achieved his first victory over the school, and in which Mirandy had been seized with her desperate passion for him, that she told him about it. Not in words. We do not allow *that* in the most civilized countries, and still less would it be tolerated in Hoopole County. But Mirandy told the master the fact that she was in love with him, though no word passed her lips. She walked by him from school. She cast at him what are commonly called sheep's-eyes. Ralph thought them more like calf's eyes. She changed the whole tone of her voice. She whined ordinarily. Now she whimpered. And so by ogling him, by blushing at him, by tittering at him, by giggling at him, by snickering at him, by simpering at him, by making herself tenfold more a fool even than nature had made her, she managed to convey to the dismayed soul of the young teacher the frightful intelligence that he was loved by the richest, the ugliest, the silliest, the coarsest, and the most entirely contemptible girl in Flat Creek district.

Ralph sat by the fire the next morning trying to read a few minutes before school-time, while the boys were doing the chores and the bound girl was milking the cows, with no one in the room but the old woman. She was generally as silent as Bud, but now she seemed for some unaccountable reason disposed to talk. She had sat down on the broad hearth to have her usual morning smoke; the poplar table, adorned by no cloth, stood in the middle of the floor; the unwashed blue teacups sat in the unwashed blue saucers; the unwashed blue plates kept company with the begrimed blue pitcher. The dirty skillets by the fire were kept in countenance by the dirtier pots, and the ashes were drifted and strewn over the hearth-stones in a most picturesque way.

"You see," said the old woman, knocking the residuum from her cob pipe, and chafing some dry leaf between her withered hands preparatory to filling it again, "you see, Mr. Hartsook, my ole man's purty well along in the world. He's got a right smart lot of this world's plunder,[1] one way

---

[1] This word *plunder* is probably from Pennsylvania, as it is exactly equivalent to the German word *plunder*, in the sense of household effects, the original meaning of the word in German. Any kind of baggage may be called *plunder*, but the most accepted sense is household goods. It is quite seriously used. I have seen bills of lading on the Western waters certifying that A. B. had shipped " 1 lot of plunder;" that is, household goods. It is here used figuratively for goods in general.

and another." And while she stuffed the tobacco
into her pipe Ralph wondered why she should mention it to him. "You see, we moved in here nigh
upon twenty-five years ago. 'Twas when my Jack,
him as died afore Bud was born, was a baby. Bud'll
be twenty-one the fif' of next June."

Here Mrs. Means stopped to rake a live coal out
of the fire with her skinny finger, and then to carry
it in her skinny palm to the bowl—or to the *hole*—
of her cob pipe. When she got the smoke a-going,
she proceeded:

"You see, this yere bottom land was all Congress
land[1] in them there days, and it sold for a dollar
and a quarter, and I says to my ole man, 'Jack,'
says I, 'Jack, do you git a plenty while you're
a-gittin'. Git a plenty while you're a-gittin',' says I,
'fer 'twon't never be no cheaper'n 'tis now,' and it
ha'n't been; I knowed 'twouldn't," and Mrs. Means
took the pipe from her mouth to indulge in a good
chuckle at the thought of her financial shrewdness.
" 'Git a plenty while you're a-gittin',' says I. I
could see, you know, they was a powerful sight of
money in Congress land. That's what made me say,
'Git a plenty while you're a-gittin'.' And Jack,
he's wuth lots and gobs of money, all made out of
Congress land. Jack didn't git rich by hard work.
Bless you, no! Not him. That a'n't his way.
Hard work a'n't, you know. 'Twas that air six
hundred dollars he got along of me, all salted down

---

[1] *Congress land* was the old designation for land owned by the government.
Under the Confederation, the Congress was the government, and the forms of
speech seem to have long retained the notion that what belonged to the United
States was the property of Congress.

into Flat Crick bottoms at a dollar and a quarter a' acre, and 'twas my sayin' 'Git a plenty while you're a gittin' ' as done it." And here the old ogre laughed, or grinned horribly, at Ralph, showing her few straggling, discolored teeth.

Then she got up and knocked the ashes out of her pipe, and laid the pipe away and walked round in front of Ralph. After adjusting the chunks[1] so that the fire would burn, she turned her yellow face toward Ralph, and scanning him closely came out with the climax of her speech in the remark: "You see as how, Mr. Hartsook, the man what gits my Mirandy'll do well. Flat Crick land's wuth nigh upon a hundred a' acre."

This gentle hint came near knocking Ralph down. Had Flat Creek land been worth a hundred times a hundred dollars an acre, and had he owned five hundred times Means's five hundred acres, he would have given it all just at that moment to have annihilated the whole tribe of Meanses. Except Bud. Bud was a giant, but a good-natured one. He thought he would except Bud from the general destruction. As for the rest, he mentally pictured to himself the pleasure of attending their funerals. There was one thought, however, between him and

---

[1] The commonest use of the word *chunk* in the old days was for the ends of the sticks of cord-wood burned in the great fireplaces. As the sticks burned in two, the chunks fell down or rolled back on the wall side of the andirons. By putting the chunks together, a new fire was set a-going without fresh wood. This use of the word is illustrated in a folk-rhyme or nursery jingle of the country which has neither sense nor elegance to recommend it:

> "Old Mother Hunk
> She got drunk
> And fell in the fire
> And kicked up a chunk."

despair. He felt confident that the cordiality, the intensity, and the persistency of his dislike of Sis Means were such that he should never inherit a foot of the Flat Creek bottoms.

But what about Bud? What if he joined the conspiracy to marry him to this weak-eyed, weak-headed wood-nymph, or backwoods nymph?

If Ralph felt it a misfortune to be loved by Mirandy Means, he found himself almost equally unfortunate in having incurred the hatred of the meanest boy in school. "Hank" Banta, low-browed, smirky, and crafty, was the first sufferer by Ralph's determination to use corporal punishment, and so Henry Banta, who was a compound of deceit and resentment, never lost an opportunity to annoy the young school-master, who was obliged to live perpetually on his guard against his tricks.

One morning, as Ralph walked toward the school-house, he met little Shocky. What the boy's first name or last name was the teacher did not know. He had given his name as Shocky, and all the teacher knew was that he was commonly called Shocky, that he was an orphan, that he lived with a family named Pearson over in Rocky Hollow, and that he was the most faithful and affectionate child in the school. On this morning that I speak of, Ralph had walked toward the school early to avoid the company of Mirandy. But not caring to sustain his dignity longer than was necessary, he loitered along the road, admiring the trunks of the maples, and picking up a beech-nut now and then. Just as he was about to go on toward the school, he caught sight of little Shocky running swiftly toward him, but looking from side to side, as if afraid of being seen.

"Well, Shocky, what is it?" and Ralph put his hand kindly on the great bushy head of white hair from which came Shocky's nickname. Shocky had to pant a minute.

"Why, Mr. Hartsook," he gasped, scratching his head, "they's a pond down under the schoolhouse," and here Shocky's breath gave out entirely for a minute.

"Yes, Shocky, I know that. What about it? The trustees haven't come to fill it up, have they?"

"Oh! no, sir; but Hank Banta, you know——" and Shocky took another breathing spell, standing as close to Ralph as he could, for poor Shocky got all his sunshine from the master's presence.

"Has Henry fallen in and got a ducking, Shocky?"

"Oh! no, sir; he wants to git you in, you see."

"Well, I won't go in, though, Shocky."

"But, you see, he's been and gone and pulled back the board that you have to step on to git ahind your desk; he's been and gone and pulled back the board so as you can't help a-tippin' it up, and a-sowsin' right in ef you step there."

"And so you came to tell me." There was a huskiness in Ralph's voice. He had, then, one friend in Flat Creek district—poor little Shocky. He put his arm around Shocky just a moment, and then told him to hasten across to the other road, so as to come back to the schoolhouse in a direction at right angles to the master's approach. But the caution was not needed. Shocky had taken care to leave in that way, and was altogether too cunning to be seen coming down the road with Mr. Hartsook. But after he got over the fence to go through the "sugar camp" (or sugar *orchard*, as they say at the East), he stopped and turned back once or twice, just to catch one more smile from Ralph. And then he hied away through the tall trees, a very happy boy, kicking and ploughing the brown leaves before him in his perfect delight, saying over and over again: "How he looked at me! how he did look!" And when Ralph came up to the schoolhouse door, there was Shocky sauntering along from the other direction, throwing bits of limestone at fence rails, and smiling still clear down to his shoes at thought of the master's kind words.

"What a quare boy Shocky is!" remarked Betsey Short, with a giggle. "He just likes to wander round alone. I see him a-comin' out of the sugar camp just now. He's been in there half an hour." And Betsey giggled again; for Betsey Short could giggle on slighter provocation than any other girl on Flat Creek.

When Ralph Hartsook, with the quiet, dogged tread that he was cultivating, walked into the schoolroom, he took great care not to seem to see the trap set for him; but he carelessly stepped over the board that had been so nicely adjusted. The boys who were Hank's confidants in the plot were very busy over their slates, and took pains not to show their disappointment.

The morning session wore on without incident.

Ralph several times caught two people looking at him. One was Mirandy. Her weak and watery eyes stole loving glances over the top of her spelling-book, which she would not study. Her looks made Ralph's spirits sink to forty below zero, and congeal.

But on one of the backless little benches that sat in the middle of the schoolroom was little Shocky, who also cast many love glances at the young master; glances as grateful to his heart as Mirandy's ogling—he was tempted to call it ogring—was hateful.

"Look at Shocky," giggled Betsey Short, behind her slate. "He looks as if he was a-goin' to eat the master up, body and soul."

And so the forenoon wore on as usual, and those who laid the trap had forgotten it, themselves. The morning session was drawing to a close. The fire in the great old fire-place had burnt low. The flames, which seemed to Shocky to be angels, had disappeared, and now the bright coals, which had played the part of men and women and houses in Shocky's fancy, had taken on a white and downy covering of ashes, and the great half-burnt back-log lay there smouldering like a giant asleep in a snow-drift. Shocky longed to wake him up.

As for Henry Banta, he was too much bothered to get the answer to a "sum" he was doing, to remember anything about his trap. In fact, he had quite forgotten that half an hour ago in the all-absorbing employment of drawing ugly pictures on his slate and coaxing Betsey Short to giggle by showing them slyly across the schoolroom. Once or twice Ralph had been attracted to Betsey's extraordinary fits of giggling, and had come so near to catching Hank that the boy thought it best not to run any further risk of the beech switches, four or five feet long, laid up behind the master in sight of the school as a prophylactic. Hence his application just now to his "sum" in long division, and hence his puzzled look, for, idler that he was, his "sums" did not solve themselves easily. As usual in such cases, he came up in front of the master's desk to have the difficulty explained. He had to wait a minute until Ralph got through with showing Betsey Short, who had been seized with a studying fit, and who could hardly give any attention to the teacher's explanations, she did want to giggle so much! Not at anything in particular, but just at things in general.

While Ralph was "doing" Betsey's "sum" for her, he was solving a much more difficult question. A plan had flashed upon him, but the punishment seemed a severe one. He gave it up once or twice, but he remembered how turbulent the Flat Creek elements were; and had he not inly resolved to be as unrelenting as a bulldog? He fortified himself by recalling again the oft-remembered remark of Bud, "Ef Bull wunst takes a holt, heaven and yarth can't make him let go." And so he resolved to give Hank and the whole school one good lesson.

"Just step round behind me, Henry, and you can see how I do this," said Ralph.

Hank was entirely off his guard, and, with his eyes fixed upon the slate on the teacher's desk, he sidled round upon the broad loose board misplaced by his own hand, and in an instant the other end of the board rose up in the middle of the schoolroom, almost striking Shocky in the face, while Henry Banta went down into the ice-cold water beneath the school-house.

"Why, Henry!" cried Ralph, jumping to his feet with well-feigned surprise. "How *did* this happen?" and he helped the dripping fellow out and seated him by the fire.

Betsey Short giggled.

Shocky was so tickled that he could hardly keep his seat.

The boys who were in the plot looked very serious indeed.

Ralph made some remarks by way of improving the occasion. He spoke strongly of the utter meanness of the one who could play so heartless a trick on a schoolmate. He said that it was as much thieving to get your fun at the expense of another as to steal his money. And while he talked, all eyes were turned on Hank—all except the eyes of Mirandy Means. They looked simperingly at Ralph. All the rest looked at Hank. The fire had made his face very red. Shocky noticed that. Betsey Short noticed it, and giggled. The master wound up with an appropriate quotation from Scripture. He said that the person who displaced that board had better not be encouraged by the success—he said *success* with a curious emphasis—of the present experiment to attempt another trick of the kind. For it was set down in the Bible that if a man dug a pit for the feet of another he would be very likely to fall in it himself. Which made all the pupils look solemn, except Betsey Short, who giggled. And Shocky wanted to. And Mirandy cast an expiring look at Ralph. And if the teacher was not love-sick, he certainly was sick of Mirandy's love.

When school was "let out," Ralph gave Hank every caution that he could about taking cold, and even lent him his overcoat, very much against Hank's will. For Hank had obstinately refused to go home before the school was dismissed.

Then the master walked out in a quiet and sub-dued way to spend the noon recess in the woods, while Shocky watched his retreating footsteps with loving admiration. And the pupils not in the secret canvassed the question of who moved the board. Bill Means said he'd bet Hank did it, which set Betsey Short off in an uncontrollable giggle. And Shocky listened innocently.

But that night Bud said slyly: "Thunder and lightning! what a manager you *air*, Mr. Hartsook!" To which Ralph returned no reply except a friendly smile. Muscle paid tribute to brains that time.

But Ralph had no time for exultation; for just here came the spelling-school.

CHAPTER IV

SPELLING DOWN THE MASTER

"I 'LOW," said Mrs. Means, as she stuffed the tobacco into her cob pipe after supper on that eventful
Wednesday evening: "I 'low they'll app'int the
Squire to gin out the words to-night. They mos'
always do, you see, kase he's the peartest[1] *ole* man
in this deestrick; and I 'low some of the young fellers
would have to git up and dust ef they would keep up
to him. And he uses sech remarkable smart words.
He speaks so polite, too. But laws! don't I remember
when he was poarer nor Job's turkey? Twenty year
ago, when he come to these 'ere diggin's, that air
Squire Hawkins was a poar Yankee schoolmaster,
that said 'pail' instid of bucket, and that called a
cow a 'caow,' and that couldn't tell to save his
gizzard what we meant by *'low*[2] and by *right*

---

[1] *Peart* or peert is only another form of the old word *pert*—probably an older
form. Bartlett cites an example of *peart* as far back as Sir Philip Sidney; and
Halliwell finds it in various English dialects. Davies, afterward president of
Princeton College, describes Dr. Lardner, in 1754, as "a little pert old gent."
I do not know that Dr. Davies pronounced his *pert* as though it were *peart*, but
he uses it in the sense it has in the text, viz., bright-witted, intelligent. The
general sense of *peart* is lively, either in body or mind.

[2] Mr. Lowell suggested to me in 1869 that this word *'low* has no kinship with
allow, but is an independent word for which he gave a Low Latin original of
similar sound. I have not been able to trace any such word, but Mr. Lowell had
so much linguistic knowledge of the out-of-the-way sort that it may be worth
while to record his impression. Bartlett is wrong in defining this word, as he is
usually in his attempts to explain dialect outside of New England. It does not
mean "to declare, assert, maintain," etc. It is nearly the equivalent of *guess* in
the Northern and Middle States, and of *reckon* in the South. It agrees precisely

30

smart.[1] But he's larnt our ways now, an' he's jest as civilized as the rest of us. You would-n know he'd ever
been a Yankee. He didn't stay poar long. Not he. He
jest married a right rich girl! He! he!" And the old
woman grinned at Ralph, and then at Mirandy, and
then at the rest, until Ralph shuddered. Nothing
was so frightful to him as to be fawned on by this
grinning ogre, whose few lonesome, blackish teeth
seemed ready to devour him. "He didn't stay poar,
you bet a hoss!" and with this the coal was deposited
on the pipe, and the lips began to crack like parch-
ment as each puff of smoke escaped. "He married
rich, you see," and here another significant look at
the young master, and another fond look at Mirandy,
as she puffed away reflectively. "His wife hadn't
no book-larnin'. She'd been through the spellin'-
book wunst, and had got as fur as 'asperity' on it a
second time. But she couldn't read a word when she

with the New England *calk'late.* Like all the rest of these words it may have a
strong sense by irony. When a man says, "I 'low that is a purty peart sort of a
hoss," he understates for the sake of emphasis. It is rarely or never *allow,* but
simply *'low.* In common with *calk'late,* it has sometimes a sense of purpose or
expectation, as when a man says, "I 'low to go to town to-morry."

[1] No phrase of the Hoosier and Southwestern dialect is such a stumbling-block
to the outsider as *right smart.* The writer from the North or East will generally
use it wrongly. Mrs. Stowe says, "I sold right smart of eggs," but the Hoosier
woman as I knew her would have said "a right smart lot of eggs" or "a right
smart of eggs," using the article and understanding the noun. A farmer omitting
the preposition boasts of having "raised right smart corn" this year. No expression could have a more vague sense than this. In the early settlement of
Minnesota it was a custom of the land officers to require a residence of about ten
days on "a claim" in order to the establishment of a pre-emption right. One of
the receivers at a land office under Buchanan's administration was a German of
much intelligence who was very sensitive regarding his knowledge of English.
"How long has the claimant lived on his claim?" he demanded of a Hoosier
witness. "Oh, a right smart while," was the reply. The receiver had not the
faintest notion of the meaning of the answer, but fearing to betray his ignorance
of English he allowed the land to be entered, though the claimant had spent but
about two hours in residing on his quarter-section.

was married, and never could. She warn't overly smart. She hadn't hardly got the sense the law allows. But schools was skase in them air days, and, besides, book-larnin' don't do no good to a woman. Makes her stuck up. I never knowed but one gal in my life as had ciphered into fractions, and she was so dog-on stuck up that she turned up her nose one night at a apple-peelin' bekase I tuck a sheet off the bed to splice out the table-cloth, which was ruther short. And the sheet was mos' clean too. Had-n been slep on more'n wunst or twicet. But I was goin' fer to say that when Squire Hawkins married Virginny Gray he got a heap o' money, or, what's the same thing mostly, a heap o' good land. And that's better'n book-larnin', says I. Ef a gal had gone clean through all eddication, and got to the rule of three itself, that would-n buy a feather-bed. Squire Hawkins jest put eddication agin the gal's farm, and traded even, an' ef ary one of 'em got swindled, I never heerd no complaints."

And here she looked at Ralph in triumph, her hard face splintering into the hideous semblance of a smile. And Mirandy cast a blushing, gushing, all-imploring, and all-confiding look on the young master.

"I say, ole woman," broke in old Jack, "I say, wot is all this 'ere spoutin' about the Square fer?" and old Jack, having bit off an ounce of "pigtail," returned the plug to his pocket.

As for Ralph, he fell into a sort of terror. He had a guilty feeling that this speech of the old lady's had somehow committed him beyond recall to

Mirandy. He did not see visions of breach-of-promise suits. But he trembled at the thought of an avenging big brother.

"Hanner, you kin come along, too, ef you're a mind, when you git the dishes washed," said Mrs. Means to the bound girl, as she shut and latched the back door. The Means family had built a new house in front of the old one, as a sort of advertisement of bettered circumstances, an eruption of shoddy feeling; but when the new building was completed, they found themselves unable to occupy it for anything else than a lumber-room, and so, except a parlor which Mirandy had made an effort to furnish a little (in hope of the blissful time when somebody should "set up" with her of evenings), the new building was almost unoccupied, and the family went in and out through the back door, which, indeed, was the front door also, for, according to a curious custom, the "front" of the house was placed toward the south, though the "big road" (Hoosier for *highway*) ran along the north-west side, or, rather, past the north-west corner of it.

When the old woman had spoken thus to Hannah and had latched the door, she muttered, "That gal don't never show no gratitude fer favors;" to which Bud rejoined that he didn't think she had no great sight to be pertickler thankful fer. To which Mrs. Means made no reply, thinking it best, perhaps, not to wake up her dutiful son on so interesting a theme as her treatment of Hannah. Ralph felt glad that he was this evening to go to another boarding place. He should not hear the rest of the controversy.

Ralph walked to the schoolhouse with Bill. They were friends again. For when Hank Banta's ducking and his dogged obstinacy in sitting in his wet clothes had brought on a serious fever, Ralph had called together the big boys, and had said: "We must take care of one another, boys. Who will volunteer to take turns sitting up with Henry?" He put his own name down, and all the rest followed.

"William Means and myself will sit up to-night," said Ralph. And poor Bill had been from that moment the teacher's friend. He was chosen to be Ralph's companion. He was Puppy Means no longer! Hank could not be conquered by kindness, and the teacher was made to feel the bitterness of his resentment long after. But Bill Means was for the time entirely placated, and he and Ralph went to spelling-school together.

Every family furnished a candle. There were yellow dips and white dips, burning, smoking, and flaring. There was laughing, and talking, and giggling, and simpering, and ogling, and flirting, and courting. What a full-dress party is to Fifth Avenue, a spelling-school is to Hoopole County. It is an occasion which is metaphorically inscribed with this legend: "Choose your partners." Spelling is only a blind in Hoopole County, as is dancing on Fifth Avenue. But as there are some in society who love dancing for its own sake, so in Flat Creek district there were those who loved spelling for its own sake, and who, smelling the battle from afar, had come to try their skill in this tournament, hoping to freshen the laurels they had won in their school-days.

"I 'low," said Mr. Means, speaking as the principal school trustee, "I 'low our friend the Square is jest the man to boss this 'ere consarn to-night. Ef nobody objects, I'll app'int him. Come, Square, don't be bashful. Walk up to the trough, fodder or no fodder, as the man said to his donkey."

There was a general giggle at this, and many of the young swains took occasion to nudge the girls alongside them, ostensibly for the purpose of making them see the joke, but really for the pure pleasure of nudging. The Greeks figured Cupid as naked, probably because he wears so many disguises that they could not select a costume for him.

The Squire came to the front. Ralph made an inventory of the agglomeration which bore the name of Squire Hawkins, as follows:

1. A swallow-tail coat of indefinite age, worn only on state occasions, when its owner was called to figure in his public capacity. Either the Squire had grown too large or the coat too small.

2. A pair of black gloves, the most phenomenal, abnormal, and unexpected apparition conceivable in Flat Creek district, where the preachers wore no coats in the summer, and where a black glove was never seen except on the hands of the Squire.

3. A wig of that dirty, waxen color so common to wigs. This one showed a continual inclination to slip off the owner's smooth, bald pate, and the Squire had frequently to adjust it. As his hair had been red, the wig did not accord with his face, and the hair ungrayed was doubly discordant with a countenance shrivelled by age.

4. A semicircular row of whiskers hedging the edge of the jaw and chin. These were dyed a frightful dead-black, such a color as belonged to no natural hair or beard that ever existed. At the roots there was a quarter of an inch of white, giving the whiskers the appearance of having been stuck on.

5. A pair of spectacles "with tortoise-shell rim." Wont to slip off.

6. A glass eye, purchased of a peddler, and differing in color from its natural mate, perpetually getting out of focus by turning in or out.

7. A set of false teeth, badly fitted, and given to bobbing up and down.

8. The Squire proper, to whom these patches were loosely attached.

It is an old story that a boy wrote home to his father begging him to come West, because "mighty mean men get into office out here." But Ralph concluded that some Yankees had taught school in Hoopole County who would not have held a high place in the educational institutions of Massachusetts. Hawkins had some New England idioms, but they were well overlaid by a Western pronunciation.

"Ladies and gentlemen," he began, shoving up his spectacles, and sucking his lips over his white teeth to keep them in place, "ladies and gentlemen, young men and maidens, raley I'm obleeged to Mr. Means fer this honor," and the Squire took both hands and turned the top of his head round half an inch. Then he adjusted his spectacles. Whether he was obliged to Mr. Means for the honor of being compared to a donkey was not clear. "I feel in the inmost compartments of my animal spirits a most happifying sense of the success and futility of all my endeavors to sarve the people of Flat Creek deestrick, and the people of Tomkins township, in my weak way and manner." This burst of eloquence was delivered with a constrained air and an apparent sense of a danger that he, Squire Hawkins, might fall to pieces in his weak way and manner, and of the success and futility of all attempts at reconstruction. For by this time the ghastly pupil of the left eye, which was black, was looking away round to the left, while the little blue one on the right twinkled cheerfully toward the front. The front teeth would drop down so that the Squire's mouth was kept nearly closed, and his words whistled through.

"I feel as if I could be grandiloquent on this interesting occasion," twisting his scalp round, "but raley I must forego any such exertions. It is spelling you want. Spelling is the corner-stone, the grand, underlying subterfuge, of a good eddication. I put the spellin'-book prepared by the great Daniel Webster alongside the Bible. I do, raley. I think I may put it ahead of the Bible. For if it wurn't fer spellin'-books and sich occasions as these, where would the Bible be? I should like to know. The man who got up, who compounded this work of inextricable valoo was a benufactor to the whole human race or any other." Here the spectacles fell off. The Squire replaced them in some confusion, gave the top of his head another twist, and felt of his glass eye, while poor Shocky stared in wonder, and Betsey Short rolled from side to side in the effort to suppress her giggle. Mrs. Means and the other old ladies looked the applause they could not speak.

"I app'int Larkin Lanham and Jeems Buchanan fer captings," said the Squire. And the two young men thus named took a stick and tossed it from hand to hand to decide which should have the "first choice." One tossed the stick to the other, who held it fast just where he happened to catch it. Then the first placed his hand above the second, and so the hands were alternately changed to the top. The one who held the stick last without room for the other to take hold had gained the lot. This was tried three times. As Larkin held the stick twice out of three times, he had the choice. He hesitated a moment. Everybody looked toward tall Jim Phillips. But Larkin was fond of a venture on unknown seas, and so he said, "I take the master," while a buzz of surprise ran round the room, and the captain of the other side, as if afraid his opponent would withdraw the choice, retorted quickly, and with a little smack of exultation and defiance in his voice, "And *I* take Jeems Phillips."

And soon all present, except a few of the old folks, found themselves ranged in opposing hosts, the poor spellers lagging in, with what grace they could, at the foot of the two divisions. The Squire opened his spelling-book and began to give out the words to the two captains, who stood up and spelled against each other. It was not long until Larkin spelled "really" with one *l*, and had to sit down in confusion, while a murmur of satisfaction ran through the ranks of the opposing forces. His own side bit their lips. The slender figure of the young teacher took the place of the fallen leader, and the excitement made the house very quiet. Ralph dreaded the loss of prestige he would suffer if he should be easily spelled down. And at the moment of rising he saw in the darkest corner the figure of a well-dressed young man sitting in the shadow. Why should his evil genius haunt him? But by a strong effort he turned his attention away from Dr. Small, and listened carefully to the words which the Squire did not pronounce very distinctly, spelling them with extreme deliberation. This gave him an air of hesitation which disappointed those on his own side. They wanted him to spell with a dashing assurance. But he did not begin a word until he had mentally felt his way through it. After ten minutes of spelling hard words Jeems Buchanan, the captain on the other side, spelled "atrocious" with an *s* instead of a *c*, and subsided, his first choice, Jeems Phillips, coming up against the teacher. This brought the excitement to fever-heat. For though Ralph was chosen first, it was entirely on trust, and most of the company were disappointed. The champion who now stood up against the school-master was a famous speller.

Jim Phillips was a tall, lank, stoop-shouldered fellow who had never distinguished himself in any other pursuit than spelling. Except in this one art of spelling he was of no account. He could not catch well or bat well in ball. He could not throw well enough to make his mark in that famous Western game of bull-pen. He did not succeed well in any study but that of Webster's Elementary. But in that he was—to use the usual Flat Creek locution —in that he was "a hoss." This genius for spelling is in some people a sixth sense, a matter of intuition. Some spellers are born, and not made, and their facility reminds one of the mathematical prodigies that crop out every now and then to bewilder the world. Bud Means, foreseeing that Ralph would be pitted against Jim Phillips, had warned his friend that Jim could "spell like thunder and lightning," and that it "took a powerful smart speller" to beat him, for he knew "a heap of spelling-book." To have "spelled down the master" is next thing to having whipped the biggest bully in Hoopole County, and Jim had "spelled down" the last three masters. He divided the hero-worship of the district with Bud Means.

For half an hour the Squire gave out hard words. What a blessed thing our crooked orthography is! Without it there could be no spelling-schools. As Ralph discovered his opponent's mettle he became more and more cautious. He was now satisfied that Jim would eventually beat him. The fellow evidently knew more about the spelling-book than old Noah Webster himself. As he stood there, with his dull face and long sharp nose, his hands behind his back, and his voice spelling infallibly, it seemed to Hartsook that his superiority must lie in his nose. Ralph's cautiousness answered a double purpose; it enabled him to tread surely, and it was mistaken by Jim for weakness. Phillips was now confident that he should carry off the scalp of the fourth schoolmaster before the evening was over. He spelled eagerly, confidently, brilliantly. Stoop-shouldered as he was, he began to straighten up. In the minds of all the company the odds were in his favor. He saw this, and became ambitious to distinguish himself by spelling without giving the matter any thought.

Ralph always believed that he would have been speedily defeated by Phillips had it not been for two thoughts which braced him. The sinister shadow of young Dr. Small sitting in the dark corner by the water-bucket nerved him. A victory over Phillips was a defeat to one who wished only ill to the young schoolmaster. The other thought that kept his pluck alive was the recollection of Bull. He approached a word as Bull approached the raccoon. He did not take hold until he was sure of his game. When he took hold, it was with a quiet assurance of success. As Ralph spelled in this dogged way for half an hour the hardest words the Squire could find, the excitement steadily rose in all parts of the house, and Ralph's friends even ventured to whisper that "maybe Jim had cotched his match, after all!"

But Phillips never doubted of his success.

"Theodolite," said the Squire.

"T-h-e, the, o-d, od, theod, o, theodo, l-y-t-e, the-odolite," spelled the champion.

"Next," said the Squire, nearly losing his teeth in his excitement. Ralph spelled the word slowly and correctly, and the conquered champion sat down in confusion. The excitement was so great for some minutes that the spelling was suspended. Everybody in the house had shown sympathy with one or the other of the combatants, except the silent shadow in the corner. It had not moved during the contest, and did not show any interest now in the result.

"Gewhilliky crickets! Thunder and lightning! Licked him all to smash!" said Bud, rubbing his hands on his knees. "That beats my time all holler!"

And Betsey Short giggled until her tuck-comb fell out, though she was on the defeated side.

Shocky got up and danced with pleasure.

But one suffocating look from the aqueous eyes of Mirandy destroyed the last spark of Ralph's pleasure in his triumph, and sent that awful below-zero feeling all through him.

"He's powerful smart, is the master," said old Jack to Mr. Pete Jones. "He'll beat the whole kit and tuck of 'em afore he's through. I know'd he was smart. That's the reason I tuck him," proceeded Mr. Means.

"Yaas, but he don't lick enough. Not nigh," answered Pete Jones. "No lickin', no larnin', says I."

It was now not so hard. The other spellers on the opposite side went down quickly under the hard words which the Squire gave out. The master had mowed down all but a few, his opponents had given up the battle, and all had lost their keen interest in a contest to which there could be but one conclusion, for there were only the poor spellers

left. But Ralph Hartsook ran against a stump
where he was least expecting it. It was the Squire's
custom, when one of the smaller scholars or poorer
spellers rose to spell against the master, to give out
eight or ten easy words, that they might have some
breathing-spell before being slaughtered, and then
to give a poser or two which soon settled them. He
let them run a little, as a cat does a doomed mouse.
There was now but one person left on the opposite
side, and, as she rose in her blue calico dress, Ralph
recognized Hannah, the bound girl at old Jack
Means's. She had not attended school in the
district, and had never spelled in spelling-school
before, and was chosen last as an uncertain quan-
tity. The Squire began with easy words of two syllables, from that page of Webster, so well known
to all who ever thumbed it, as "baker," from the
word that stands at the top of the page. She spelled
these words in an absent and uninterested manner.
As everybody knew that she would have to go down
as soon as this preliminary skirmishing was over,
everybody began to get ready to go home, and already there was the buzz of preparation. Young
men were timidly asking girls if "they could see
them safe home," which was the approved formula,
and were trembling in mortal fear of "the mitten."
Presently the Squire, thinking it time to close the
contest, pulled his scalp forward, adjusted his glass
eye, which had been examining his nose long enough,
and turned over the leaves of the book to the great
words at the place known to spellers as "incompre-
hensibility," and began to give out those "words of

eight syllables with the accent on the sixth." Listless scholars now turned round, and ceased to whisper, in order to be in at the master's final triumph. But to their surprise "ole Miss Meanses' white nigger," as some of them called her in allusion to her slavish life, spelled these great words with as perfect ease as the master. Still not doubting the result, the Squire turned from place to place and selected all the hard words he could find. The school became utterly quiet, the excitement was too great for the ordinary buzz. Would "Meanses' Hanner" beat the master? beat the master that had laid out Jim Phillips? Everybody's sympathy was now turned to Hannah. Ralph noticed that even Shocky had deserted him, and that his face grew brilliant every time Hannah spelled a word. In fact, Ralph deserted himself. As he saw the fine, timid face of the girl so long oppressed flush and shine with interest; as he looked at the rather low but broad and intelligent brow and the fresh, white complexion and saw the rich, womanly nature coming to the surface under the influence of applause and sympathy—he did not want to beat. If he had not felt that a victory given would insult her, he would have missed intentionally. The bulldog, the stern, relentless setting of the will, had gone, he knew not whither. And there had come in its place, as he looked in that face, a something which he did not understand. You did not, gentle reader, the first time it came to you

The Squire was puzzled. He had given out all the

hard words in the book. He again pulled the top of his head forward. Then he wiped his spectacles and put them on. Then out of the depths of his pocket he fished up a list of words just coming into use in those days—words not in the spelling-book. He regarded the paper attentively with his blue right eye. His black left eye meanwhile fixed itself in such a stare on Mirandy Means that she shuddered and hid her eyes in her red silk handkerchief.

"Daguerreotype," sniffed the Squire. It was Ralph's turn.

"D-a-u, dau——"

"Next."

And Hannah spelled it right.

Such a buzz followed that Betsey Short's giggle could not be heard, but Shocky shouted: "Hanner beat! my Hanner spelled down the master!" And Ralph went over and congratulated her.

And Dr. Small sat perfectly still in the corner.

And then the Squire called them to order, and said: "As our friend Hanner Thomson is the only one left on her side, she will have to spell against nearly all on t'other side. I shall therefore take the liberty of procrastinating the completion of this interesting and exacting contest until to-morrow evening. I hope our friend Hanner may again carry off the cypress crown of glory. There is nothing better for us than healthful and kindly simulation."

Dr. Small, who knew the road to practice, escorted Mirandy, and Bud went home with somebody else. The others of the Means family hurried on, while Hannah, the champion, stayed behind a minute to speak to Shocky. Perhaps it was because Ralph saw that Hannah must go alone that he suddenly remembered having left something which was of no consequence, and resolved to go round by Mr. Means's and get it.

CHAPTER V

THE WALK HOME

You expect me to describe that walk. You have had enough of the Jack Meanses and the Squire Hawkinses, and the Pete Joneses, and the rest. You wish me to tell you now of this true-hearted girl and her lover; of how the silvery moonbeams came down in a shower—to use Whittier's favorite metaphor—through the maple boughs, flecking the frozen ground with light and shadow. You would have me tell of the evening star, not yet gone down, which shed its benediction on them. But I shall do no such thing. For the moon was not shining, neither did the stars give their light. The tall, black trunks of the maples swayed and shook in the wind, which moaned through their leafless boughs. Novelists always make lovers walk in the moonlight. But if love is not, as the cynics believe, all moonshine, it can at least make its own light. Moonlight is never so little needed or heeded, never so much of an impertinence, as in a love-scene. It was at the bottom of the first hollow beyond the schoolhouse that Ralph overtook the timid girl walking swiftly through the dark. He did not ask permission to walk with her. Love does not go by words, and there are times when conventionality is impossible. There are people who understand one another at once. When one soul meets another, it is not by pass-word, nor by hailing sign, nor by mysterious grip that they recognize. The subtlest freemasonry in the world is this freemasonry of the spirit.

Ralph and Hannah knew and trusted. Ralph had admired and wondered at the quiet drudge. But it was when, in the unaccustomed sunshine of praise, she spread her wings a little, that he loved her. He had seen her awake.

You, Miss Amelia, wish me to repeat all their love-talk. I am afraid you'd find it dull. Love can pipe through any kind of a reed. Ralph talked love to Hannah when he spoke of the weather, of the crops, of the spelling-school. Weather, crops, and spelling-school—these were what his words would say if reported. But below all these commonplaces there vibrated something else. One can make love a great deal better when one doesn't speak of love. Words are so poor! Tones and modulations are better. It is an old story that Whitefield could make an audience weep by his way of pronouncing the word Mesopotamia. A lover can sound the whole gamut of his affection in saying Good-morning. The solemnest engagements ever made have been without the intervention of speech.

And you, my Gradgrind friend, you think me sentimental. Two young fools they were, walking so slowly though the night was sharp, dallying under the trees, and dreaming of a heaven they could not have realized if all their wishes had been granted. Of course they were fools! Either they were fools to be so happy, or else some other people are fools not to be. After all, dear Gradgrind, let them be.

There's no harm in it. They'll get trouble enough before morning. Let them enjoy the evening. I am not sure but these lovers whom we write down fools are the only wise people, after all. Is it not wise to be happy? Let them alone.

For the first time in three years, for the first time since she had crossed the threshold of "Old Jack Means" and come under the domination of Mrs. Old Jack Means, Hannah talked cheerfully, almost gayly. It was something to have a companion to talk to. It was something to be the victor even in a spelling-match, and to be applauded even by Flat Creek. And so, chatting earnestly about the most uninteresting themes, Ralph courteously helped Hannah over the fence, and they took the usual short-cut through the "blue-grass pasture." There came up a little shower, hardly more than a sprinkle, but then it was so nice to have a shower just as they reached the box-elder tree by the spring! It was so thoughtful in Ralph to suggest that the shade of a box-elder is dense, and that Hannah might take cold! And it was so easy for Hannah to yield to the suggestion! Just as though she had not milked the cows in the open lot in the worst storms of the last three years! And just as though the house were not within a stone's-throw! Doubtless it was not prudent to stop here. But let us deal gently with them. Who would not stay in an earthy paradise ten minutes longer, even though it did make purgatory the hotter afterward? And so Hannah stayed.

"Tell me your circumstances," said Ralph, at last. "I am sure I can help you in something."

"No, no! you cannot," and Hannah's face was clouded. "No one can help me. Only time and God. I must go, Mr. Hartsook." And they walked on to the front gate in silence and in some constraint. But still in happiness.

As they came to the gate, Dr. Small pushed past them in his cool, deliberate way, and mounted his horse. Ralph bade Hannah good-night, having entirely forgotten the errand which had been his excuse to himself for coming out of his way. He hastened to his new home, the house of Mr. Pete Jones, the same who believed in the inseparableness of "lickin' and larnin'."

"You're a purty gal, a'n't you? You're a purty gal, a'n't you? *You* air! Yes, you *air!!*" and Mrs. Means seemed so impressed with Hannah's prettiness that she choked on it, and could get no further. "A purty gal! you! Yes! you air a mighty purty gal!" and the old woman's voice rose till it could have been heard half a mile. "To be a-santerin' along the big road after ten o'clock with the master! Who knows whether he's a fit man fer anybody to go with? Arter all I've been and gone and done fer you! That's the way you pay me! Disgrace me! Yes, I say disgrace me! You're a mean, deceitful thing. Stuck up bekase you spelt the master down. Ketch *me* lettin' you go to spellin'-school to-morry night! Ketch ME! Yes, ketch ME, I say!"

"Looky here, marm," said Bud, "it seems to me you're a-makin' a blamed furss about nothin'. Don't yell so's they'll hear you three or four mile. You'll have everybody 'tween here and Clifty waked up."

For Mrs. Means had become so excited over the idea of being caught allowing Hannah to go to spelling-school that she had raised her last "Ketch me!" to a perfect whoop.

"That's the way I'm treated," whimpered the old woman, who knew how to take the "injured innocence" dodge as well as anybody. "That's the way I'm treated. You allers take sides with that air hussy agin your own flesh and blood. You don't keer how much trouble I have. Not you. Not a dog-on'd bit. I may be disgraced by that air ongrateful critter, and you set right here in my own house and sass me about it. A purty fellow you air! An' me a-delvin' and a-drudgin' fer you all my born days. A purty son, a'n't you?"

Bud did not say another word. He sat in the chimney-corner and whistled "Dandy Jim from Caroline." His diversion had produced the effect he sought: for while his tender-hearted mother poured her broadside into his iron-clad feelings, Hannah had slipped up the stairs to her garret bedroom, and when Mrs. Means turned from the callous Bud to finish her assault upon the sensitive girl, she could only gnash her teeth in disappointment.

Stung by the insults to which she could not grow insensible, Hannah lay awake until the memory of that walk through the darkness came into her soul like a benediction. The harsh voice of the scold died out, and the gentle and courteous voice of Hartsook filled her soul. She recalled piece by piece the whole conversation—all the commonplace remarks about the weather; all the insignificant remarks about the crops; all the unimportant words about the spelling-school. Not for the sake of the remarks. Not for the sake of the weather. Not for the sake of the crops. Not for the sake of the spelling-school. But for the sake of the undertone. And then she traveled back over the three years of her bondage and forward over the three years to come, and fed her heart on the dim hope of rebuilding in some form the home that had been so happy. And she prayed, with more faith then ever before, for deliverance. For love brings faith. Somewhere on in the sleepless night she stood at the window. The moon was shining now, and there was the path through the pasture, and there was the fence, and there was the box-elder.

She sat there a long time. Then she saw some one come over the fence and walk to the tree, and then on toward Pete Jones's. Who could it be? She thought she recognized the figure. But she was chilled and shivering, and she crept back again into bed, and dreamed not of the uncertain days to come, but of the blessed days that were past—of a father and a mother and a brother in a happy home. But somehow the schoolmaster was there too.

CHAPTER VI

A NIGHT AT PETE JONES'S

WHEN Ralph got to Pete Jones's he found that sinister-looking individual in the act of kicking one of his many dogs out of the house.

"Come in, stranger, come in. You'll find this 'ere house full of brats, but I guess you kin kick your way around among 'em. Take a cheer. Here, git out! go to thunder with you!" And with these mild imperatives he boxed one of his boys over in one direction and one of his girls over in the other. "I believe in trainin' up children to mind when they're spoke to," he said to Ralph apologetically. But it seemed to the teacher that he wanted them to mind just a little before they were spoken to.

"P'raps you'd like a bed. Well, jest climb up the ladder on the outside of the house. Takes up a thunderin' sight of room to have a stairs inside, and we ha'n't got no room to spare. You'll find a bed in the furdest corner. My Pete's already got half of it, and you can take t'other half. Ef Pete goes to takin' his half in the middle, and tryin' to make you take yourn on both sides, jest kick him."

In this comfortless bed "in the furdest corner," Ralph found sleep out of the question. Pete took three-fourths of the bed, and Hannah took all of his thoughts. So he lay, and looked out through the cracks in the "clapboards" (as they call rough shingles in the old West) at the stars. For the clouds had now broken away. And he lay thus recounting to himself, as a miser counts the pieces that compose his hoard, every step of that road from the time he had overtaken Hannah in the hollow to the fence. Then he imagined again the pleasure of helping her over, and then he retraced the ground to the box-elder tree at the spring, and repeated to himself the conversation until he came to the part in which she said that only time and God could help her. What did she mean? What was the hidden part of her life? What was the connection between her and Shocky?

Hours wore on, and still the mind of Ralph Hartsook went back and traveled the same road, over the fence, past the box-elder, up to the inexplicable part of the conversation, and stood bewildered with the same puzzling questions about the bound girl's life.

At last he got up, drew on his clothes, and sat down on the top of the ladder, looking down over the blue-grass pasture which lay on the border between the land of Jones and the land of Means. The earth was white with moonlight. He could not sleep. Why not walk? It might enable him to sleep. And once determined on walking, he did not hesitate a moment as to the direction in which he should walk. The blue-grass pasture (was it not like unto the garden of Eden?) lay right before him. That box-elder stood just in sight. To spring over the fence and take the path down the hill and over the brook was as quickly done as decided upon.

To stand again under the box-elder, to climb again over the farther fence, and to walk down the road toward the schoolhouse was so easy and so delightful that it was done without thought. For Ralph was an eager man—when he saw no wrong in anything that proposed itself, he was wont to follow his impulse without deliberation. And this keeping company with the stars, and the memory of a delightful walk, were so much better than the commonplace Flat Creek life that he threw himself into his night excursion with enthusiasm.

At last he stood in the little hollow where he had joined Hannah. It was the very spot at which Shocky, too, had met him a few mornings before. He leaned against the fence and tried again to solve the puzzle of Hannah's troubles. For that she had troubles he did not doubt. Neither did he doubt that he could help her if he could discover what they were. But he had no clue. In the midst of his meditations he heard the thud of horses' hoofs coming down the road. Until that moment he had not felt his own loneliness. He shrank back into the fence-corner. The horsemen were galloping. There were three of them, and there was one figure that seemed familiar to Ralph. But he could not tell who it was. Neither could he remember having seen the horse, which was a sorrel with a white left forefoot and a white nose. The men noticed him and reined up a little. Why he should have been startled by the presence of these men he could not tell, but an indefinable dread seized him. They galloped on, and he stood still shivering with a nervous fear. The cold seemed to have got into his bones. He remembered that the region lying on Flat Creek and Clifty Creek had the reputation of being infested with thieves, who practiced horse-stealing and house-breaking. For ever since the day when Murrell's confederate bands were paralyzed by the death of their leader, there have still existed gangs of desperadoes in parts of Southern Indiana and Illinois, and in Iowa, Missouri, Kentucky, and the South-west. It is out of these materials that border ruffianism has grown, and the nine members of the Reno band who were hanged two or three years ago by lynch law,[1] were remains of the bad blood that came into the West in the days of Daniel Boone. Shall I not say that these bands of desperadoes still found among the "poor whitey," "dirt-eater" class are the outcroppings of the bad blood sent from England in convict-ships? Ought an old country to sow the fertile soil of a colony with such noxious seed?

Before Ralph was able to move, he heard the hoofs of another horse striking upon the hard ground in an easy pace. The rider was Dr. Small. He checked his horse in a cool way, and stool still a few seconds while he scrutinized Ralph. Then he rode on, keeping the same easy gait as before. Ralph had a superstitious horror of Henry Small. And, shuddering with cold, he crept like a thief over the fence, past the tree, through the pasture, back to Pete Jones's, never once thinking of the eyes that looked out of the window at Means's. Climbing the ladder, he

---

[1] Written in 1871.

got into bed, and shook as with the ague. He tried
to reason himself out of the foolish terror that
possessed him, but he could not.

Half an hour later he heard a latch raised. Were
the robbers breaking into the house below? He
heard a soft tread upon the floor. Should he rise
and give the alarm? Something restrained him.
He reflected that a robber would be sure to stumble
over some of the "brats." So he lay still and finally,
slumbered, only awakening when the place in
which he slept was full of the smoke of frying grease
from the room below.

At breakfast Pete Jones scowled. He was evidently angry about something. He treated Ralph
with a rudeness not to be overlooked, as if he intended to bring on a quarrel. Hartsook kept cool,
and wished he could drive from his mind all memory
of the past night. Why should men on horseback
have any significance to him? He was trying to
regard things in this way, and from a general desire
to keep on good terms with his host he went to the
stable to offer his services in helping to feed the stock.

"Don't want no saft-handed help!" was all he
got in return for his well-meant offer. But just as
he turned to leave the stable he saw what made him
tremble again. There was the same sorrel horse with
a white left forefoot and a white nose.

To shake off his nervousness, Ralph started to
school before the time. But, plague upon plagues!
Mirandy Means, who had seen him leave Pete
Jones's, started just in time to join him where he
came into the big road. Ralph was not in a good

humor after his wakeful night, and to be thus dogged by Mirandy did not help the matter. So he found himself speaking crabbedly to the daughter of the leading trustee, in spite of himself.

"Hanner's got a bad cold this mornin' from bein' out last night, and she can't come to spellin'-school to-night," began Mirandy, in her most simpering voice.

Ralph had forgotten that there was to be another spelling-school. It seemed to him an age since the orthographical conflict of the past night. This remark of Mirandy's fell upon his ear like an echo from the distant past. He had lived a lifetime since, and was not sure that he was the same man who was spelling for dear life against Jim Phillips twelve hours before. But he was sorry to hear that Hannah had a cold. It seemed to him, in his depressed state, that he was to blame for it. In fact, it seemed to him that he was to blame for a good many things. He seemed to have been committing sins in spite of himself. Broken nerves and sleepless nights often result in a morbid conscience. And what business had he to wander over this very road at two o'clock in the morning, and to see three galloping horsemen, one of them on a horse with a white left forefoot and a white nose? What business had he watching Dr. Small as he went home from the bedside of a dying patient near daylight in the morning? And because he felt guilty he felt cross with Mirandy, and to her remark about Hannah he only replied that "Hannah was a smart girl."

"Yes," said Mirandy, "Bud thinks so."

"Does he?" said Ralph.

"I should say so. What's him and her been a-courtin' fer for a year ef he didn't think she was smart? Marm don't like it; but ef Bud and her does, and they seem to, I don't see as it's marm's lookout."

When one is wretched, there is a pleasure in being entirely wretched. Ralph felt that he must have committed some unknown crime, and that some Nemesis was following him. Was Hannah deceitful? At least, if she were not, he felt sure that he could supplant Bud. But what right had he to supplant Bud?

"Did you hear the news?" cried Shocky, running out to meet him. "The Dutchman's house was robbed last night."

Ralph thought of the three men on horseback, and to save his life he could not help associating Dr. Small with them. And then he remembered the sorrel horse with the left forefoot and muzzle white, and he recalled the sound he had heard as of the lifting of a latch. And it really seemed to him that in knowing what he did he was in some sense guilty of the robbery.

CHAPTER VII

THE schoolmaster's mind was like ancient Gaul—divided into three parts. With one part he mechanically performed his school duties. With another he asked himself, What shall I do about the robbery? And with the third he debated about Bud and Hannah. For Bud was not present, and it was clear that he was angry, and there was a storm brewing. In fact, it seemed to Ralph that there was a storm brewing all round the sky. For Pete Jones was evidently angry at the thought of having been watched, and it was fair to suppose that Dr. Small was not in any better humor than usual. And so, between Bud's jealousy and revenge and the suspicion and resentment of the men engaged in the robbery at "the Dutchman's" (as the only German in the whole region was called), Ralph's excited nerves had cause for tremor. At one moment he would resolve to have Hannah at all costs. In the next his conscience would question the rightfulness of the conclusion. Then he would make up his mind to tell all he knew about the robbery. But if he told his suspicions about Small, nobody would believe him. And if he told about Pete Jones, he really could tell only enough to bring vengeance upon himself. And how could he explain his own walk through the

pasture and down the road? What business had he
being out of bed at two o'clock in the morning? The
circumstantial evidence was quite as strong against
him as against the man on the horse with the white
left forefoot and the white nose. Suspicion might
fasten on himself. And then what would be the
effect on his prospects? On the people at Lewisburg?
On Hannah? It is astonishing how much instruction
and comfort there is in a bulldog. This slender
schoolmaster, who had been all his life repressing the
animal and developing the finer nature, now found
a need of just what the bulldog had. And so, with the
thought of how his friend the dog would fight in
a desperate strait, he determined to take hold of
his difficulties as Bull took hold of the raccoon.
Moral questions he postponed for careful decision.
But for the present he set his teeth together in a
desperate, bulldog fashion, and he set his feet down
slowly, positively bulldoggedly. After a wretched
supper at Pete Jones's he found himself at the spelling-school, which, owing to the absence of Hannah,
and the excitement about the burglary, was a dull
affair. Half the evening was spent in talking in little
knots. Pete Jones had taken the afflicted "Dutchman" under his own particular supervision.

"I s'pose," said Pete, "that them air fellers what
robbed your house must a come down from Jinkins
Run. They're the blamedest set up there I ever
see."

"Ya-as," said Schroeder, "put how did Yinkins
vellers know dat I sell te medder to te Shquire,
hey? How tid Yinkins know anyting 'bout the

Shquire's bayin' me dree huntert in te hard gash—hey?"

"Some scoundrels down in these 'ere parts is a-layin' in with Jinkins Run, I'll bet a hoss," said Pete. Ralph wondered whether he'd bet the one with the white left forefoot and the white nose. "Now," said Pete, "ef I could find the feller that's a-helpin' them scoundrels rob us folks, I'd help stretch him to the nearest tree."

"So vood I," said Schroeder. "I'd shtretch him dill he baid me my dree huntert tollars pack, so I vood."

And Betsey Short, who had found the whole affair very funny, was transported with a fit of tittering at poor Schroeder's English. Ralph, fearing that his silence would excite suspicion, tried to talk. But he could not tell what he knew, and all that he said sounded so hollow and hypocritical that it made him feel guilty. And so he shut his mouth, and meditated profitably on the subject of bull-dogs. And when later he overheard the garrulous Jones declare that he'd bet a hoss he could p'int out somebody as know'd a blamed sight more'n they keerd to tell, he made up his mind that if it came to p'inting out he should try to be even with Jones.

CHAPTER VIII

THE STRUGGLE IN THE DARK

IT was a long, lonesome, fearful night that the schoolmaster passed, lying with nerves on edge and eyes wide open in that comfortless bed in the "furdest corner" of the loft of Pete Jones's house, shivering with cold, while the light snow that was falling sifted in upon the ragged patch-work quilt that covered him. Nerves broken by sleeplessness imagine many things, and for the first hour Ralph felt sure that Pete would cut his throat before morning.

And you, friend Callow, who have blunted your palate by swallowing the Cayenne pepper of the penny-dreadfuls, you wish me to make this night exciting by a hand-to-hand contest between Ralph and a robber. You would like it better if there were a trap-door. There's nothing so convenient as a trap-door, unless it be a subterranean passage. And you'd like something of that sort just here. It's so pleasant to have one's hair stand on end, you know, when one is safe from danger to one's self. But if you want each individual hair to bristle with such a "Struggle in the Dark," you can buy trap-doors and subterranean passages dirt cheap at the next news-stand. But it was, indeed, a real and terrible "Struggle in the Dark" that Ralph fought out at Pete Jones's.

When he had vanquished his fears of personal violence by reminding himself that it would be folly for Jones to commit murder in his own house, the question of Bud and Hannah took the uppermost place in his thoughts. And as the image of Hannah spelling against the master came up to him, as the memory of the walk, the talk, the box-elder tree, and all the rest took possession of him, it seemed to Ralph that his very life depended upon his securing her love. He would shut his teeth like the jaws of a bulldog, and all Bud's muscles should not prevail over his resolution and his stratagems.

It was easy to persuade himself that this was right. Hannah ought not to throw herself away on Bud Means. Men of some culture always play their conceit off against their consciences. To a man of literary habits it usually seems to be a great boon that he confers on a woman when he gives her his love. Reasoning thus, Ralph had fixed his resolution, and if the night had been shorter, or sleep possible, the color of his life might have been changed.

But some time along in the tedious hours came the memory of his childhood, the words of his mother, the old Bible stories, the aspiration after nobility of spirit, the solemn resolutions to be true to his conscience. These angels of the memory came flocking back before the animal, the bull-doggedness, had "set," as workers in plaster say. He remembered the story of David and Nathan, and it seemed to him that he, with all his abilities and ambitions and prospects, was about to rob Bud of the one ewe-lamb, the only thing he had to rejoice in in his life. In getting Hannah, he would make himself unworthy of Hannah. And then there came to him a vision of the supreme value of a true character; how it was better than success, better than to be loved, better than heaven. And how near he had been to missing it! And how certain he was, when these thoughts should fade, to miss it! He was as one fighting for a great prize who feels his strength failing and is sure of defeat.

This was the real, awful "Struggle in the Dark." A human soul fighting with heaven in sight, but certain of slipping inevitably into hell! It was the same old battle. The Image of God fought with the Image of the Devil. It was the same fight that Paul described so dramatically when he represented the Spirit as contending with the Flesh. Paul also called this dreadful something the Old Adam, and I suppose Darwin would call it the remains of the Wild Beast. But call it what you will, it is the battle that every well-endowed soul must fight at some point. And to Ralph it seemed that the final victory of the Evil, the Old Adam, the Flesh, the Wild Beast, the Devil, was certain. For, was not the pure, unconscious face of Hannah on the Devil's side? And so the battle had just as well be given up at once, for it must be lost in the end.

But to Ralph, lying there in the still darkness, with his conscience as wide awake as if it were the Day of Doom, there seemed something so terrible in this overflow of the better nature which he knew to be inevitable as soon as the voice of conscience became blunted, that he looked about for help. He did not at first think of God; but there came into his thoughts the memory of a travel-worn Galilean peasant, hungry, sleepy, weary, tempted, tried, like other men, but having a strange, divine Victory in Him by which everything evil was vanquished at His coming. He remembered how He had reached out a Hand to every helpless one, how He was the Helper of every weak one. And out of the depths of his soul he cried to the Helper, and found comfort. Not victory, but, what is better, strength. And so, without a thought of the niceties of theological distinctions, without dreaming that it was the beginning of a religious experience, he found what he needed, help. And the Helper gave His beloved sleep.

CHAPTER IX

HAS GOD FORGOTTEN SHOCKY?

"PAP wants to know ef you would spend tomorry and Sunday at our house?" said one of Squire Hawkins's girls, on the very next evening, which was Friday. The old Squire was thoughtful enough to remember that Ralph would not find it very pleasant "boarding out" all the time he was entitled to spend at Pete Jones's. For in view of the fact that Mr. Pete Jones sent seven children to the school, the "master" in Flat Creek district was bound to spend two weeks in that comfortable place, sleeping in a preoccupied bed, in the "furdest corner," with insufficient cover, under an insufficient roof, and eating floating islands of salt pork fished out of oceans of hot lard. Ralph was not slow to accept the relief offered by the hospitable justice of the peace, whose principal business seemed to be the adjustment of the pieces of which he was composed. And as Shocky traveled the same road, Ralph took advantage of the opportunity to talk with him. The master could not dismiss Hannah wholly from his mind. He would at least read the mystery of her life, if Shocky could be prevailed on to furnish the clue.

"Poor old tree!" said Shocky, pointing to a crooked and gnarled elm standing by itself in the middle of a field. For when the elm, naturally the most graceful of trees, once gets a "bad set," it can grow to be the most deformed. This solitary tree had not a single straight limb.

"Why do you say 'poor old tree'?" asked Ralph.

"'Cause it's lonesome. All its old friends is dead and chopped down, and there's their stumps a-standin' jes like grave-stones. It *must* be lonesome. Some folks says it don't feel, but I think it does. Everything seems to think and feel. See it nodding its head to them other trees in the woods, and a-wantin' to shake hands! But it can't move. I think that tree must a growed in the night."

"Why, Shocky?"

"'Cause it's so crooked," and Shocky laughed at his own conceit; "must a growed when they was no light so as it could see how to grow."

And then they walked on in silence a minute. Presently Shocky began looking up into Ralph's eyes to get a smile. "I guess that tree feels just like me. Don't you?"

"Why, how do you feel?"

"Kind o' bad and lonesome, and like as if I wanted to die, you know. Felt that way ever sence they put my father into the graveyard, and sent my mother to the poor-house and Hanner to ole Miss Means's. What kind of a place is a poorhouse? Is it a poorer place than Means's? I wish I was dead and one of them clouds was a-carryin' me and Hanner and mother up to where father's gone, you know! I wonder if God forgets all about poor folks when their father dies and their mother gits into the poor-house? Do you think He does? Seems so to me. Maybe God lost track of my father when he come away from England and crossed over the sea. Don't nobody on Flat Creek keer fer God, and I guess God don't keer fer Flat Creek. But I would, though, ef He'd git my. mother out of the poor-house and git Hanner away from Means's, and let me kiss my mother every night, you know, and sleep on my Hanner's arm, jes like I used to afore father died, you see."

Ralph wanted to speak, but he couldn't. And so Shocky, with his eyes looking straight ahead, and as if forgetting Ralph's presence, told over the thoughts that he had often talked over to the fence rails and the trees. "It was real good in Mr. Pearson to take me, wasn't it? Else I'd a been bound out tell I was twenty-one, maybe, to some mean man like Ole Means. And I a'n't but seven. And it would take me fourteen years to git twenty-one, and I never could live with my mother again after Hanner gets done her time. 'Cause, you see, Hanner'll be through in three more year, and I'll be ten and able to work, and we'll git a little place about as big as Granny Sanders's, and——"

Ralph did not hear another word of what Shocky said that afternoon. For there, right before them, was Granny Sanders's log-cabin, with its row of lofty sunflower stalks, now dead and dry, in front, with its rain-water barrel by the side of the low door, and its ash-barrel by the fence. In this cabin lived alone the old and shriveled hag whose hideousness gave her a reputation for almost supernatural knowledge. She was at once doctress and newspaper. She collected and disseminated medicinal herbs and personal gossip. She was in every regard indispensable to the intellectual life of the neighborhood. In the matter of her medical skill we cannot express an opinion, for her "yarbs" are not to be found in the pharmacopœia of science.

What took Ralph's breath was to find Dr. Small's fine, faultless horse standing at the door. What did Henry Small want to visit this old quack for?

CHAPTER X

THE DEVIL OF SILENCE

RALPH had reason to fear Small, who was a native of the same village of Lewisburg, and some five years the elder. Some facts in the doctor's life had come into Ralph's possession in such a way as to confirm life-long suspicion without giving him power to expose Small, who was firmly intrenched in the good graces of the people of the county-seat village of Lewisburg, where he had grown up, and of the little cross-roads village of Clifty, where his "shingle" now hung.

Small was no ordinary villain. He was a genius. Your ordinary hypocrite talks cant. Small talked nothing. He was the coolest, the steadiest, the most silent, the most promising boy ever born in Lewisburg. He made no pretensions. He set up no claims. He uttered no professions. He went right on and lived a life above reproach. Your vulgar hypocrite makes long prayers in prayer-meeting. Small did nothing of the sort. He sat still in prayer-meeting, and listened to the elders as a modest young man should. Your commonplace hypocrite boasts. Small never alluded to himself, and thus a consummate egotist got credit for modesty. It is but an indifferent trick for a hypocrite to make temperance speeches. Dr. Small did not even belong to a temperance society. But he could never be persuaded to drink even so much as a cup of tea. There was something sublime in the quiet voice with which he would say, "Cold water, if you please," to a lady tempting him with smoking coffee on a cold morning. There was no exultation, no sense of merit in the act. Everything was done in a modest and matter-of-course way beautiful to behold. And his face was a neutral tint. Neither face nor voice expressed anything. Only a keen reader of character might have asked whether all there was in that eye could live contented with this cool, austere, self-contained life; whether there would not be somewhere a volcanic eruption. But if there was any sea of molten lava beneath the world did not discover it. Wild boys were sick of having Small held up to them as the most immaculate of men.[1]

Ralph had failed to get two schools for which he had applied, and had attributed both failures to certain shrugs of Dr. Small. And now, when he found Small at the house of Granny Sanders, the center of intelligence as well as of ignorance for the neighborhood, he trembled. Not that Small would say anything. He never said anything. He damned people by a silence worse than words.

Granny Sanders was not a little flattered by the visit.

"Why, doctor, howdy, howdy! Come in, take a cheer. I am glad to see you. I 'lowed you'd come.

---

[1] The original from which this character was drawn is here described accurately. The author now knows that such people are not to be put into books. They are not realistic enough.

Old Dr. Flounder used to say he larnt lots o' things of me. But most of the doctors sence hez been kinder stuck up, you know. But I know'd you fer a man of intelligence."

Meantime, Small, by his grave silence and attention, had almost smothered the old hag with flattery. "Many's the case I've cured with yarbs and things. Nigh upon twenty year ago they was a man lived over on Wild Cat Run as had a breakin' out on his side. 'Twas the left side, jes below the waist. Doctor couldn't do nothin'. 'Twas Doctor Peacham. He never would have nothin' to do with 'ole woman's cures.' Well, the man was goin' to die. Everybody seed that. And they come a-drivin' away over here all the way from the Wild Cat. Think of that air! I never was so flustered. But as soon as I laid eyes on that air man, I says, says I, that air man, says I, has got the shingles, says I. I know'd the minute I seed it. And if they'd gone clean around, nothing could a saved him. I says, says I, git me a black cat. So I jist killed a black cat, and let the blood run all over the swellin'. I tell you, doctor, they's nothin' like it. That man was well in a month."

"Did you use the blood warm?" asked Small, with a solemnity most edifying.

These were almost the only words he had uttered since he entered the cabin.

"Laws, yes; I jest let it run right out of the cat's tail onto the breakin'-out. And fer airesipelus, I don't know nothin' so good as the blood of a black hen."

"How old?" asked the doctor.

"There you showed yer science, doctor! They's no power in a pullet. The older the black hen the better. And you know the cure fer rheumatiz?" And here the old woman got down a bottle of grease. "That's ile from a black dog. Ef it's rendered right, it'll knock the hind sights off of any rheumatiz you ever see. But it must be rendered in the dark of the moon. Else a black dog's ile a'n't worth no more nor a white one's."

And all this time Small was smelling of the un-corked bottle, taking a little on his finger and feel-ing of it, and thus feeling his way to the heart—drier than her herbs—of the old witch. And then he went round the cabin gravely, lifting each separate bunch of dried yarbs from its nail, smelling of it, and then, by making an interrogation-point of his silent face, he managed to get a lecture from her on each article in her *materia medica*, with the most marvelous stories illustrative of their virtues. When the Granny had got her fill of his silent flattery, he was ready to carry forward his main purpose.

There was something weird about this silent man's ability to turn the conversation as he chose to have it go. Sitting by the Granny's tea-table, nibbling corn-bread while he drank his glass of water, having declined even her sassafras, he ceased to stimulate her medical talk and opened the vein of gossip. Once started, Granny Sanders was sure to allude to the robbery. And once on the robbery the doctor's course was clear.

"I 'low somebody not fur away is in this 'ere business!"

Not by a word, nor even by a nod, but by some motion of the eyelids, perhaps, Small indicated that he agreed with her.

"Who d'ye s'pose 'tis?"

But Dr. Small was not in the habit of supposing. He moved his head in a quiet way, just the least perceptible bit, but so that the old creature understood that he could give light if he wanted to.

"I dunno anybody that's been 'bout here long as could be suspected."

Another motion of the eyelids indicated Small's agreement with this remark.

"They a'n't nobody come in here lately 'ceppin' the master."

Small looked vacantly at the wall.

"But I 'low he's allers bore a tip-top character."

The doctor was too busy looking at his corn-bread to answer this remark even by a look.

"But I think these oversmart young men'll bear looking arter, *I* do."

Dr. Small raised his eyes and let them *shine* an assent. That was all.

"Shouldn't wonder ef our master was overly fond of gals."

Doctor looks down at his plate.

"Had plenty of sweethearts afore he walked home with Hanner Thomson t'other night, I'll bet."

Did Dr. Small shrug his shoulder? Granny thought she detected a faint motion of the sort, but she could not be sure.

"And I think as how that a feller what trifles with gals' hearts and then runs off ten miles, maybe

a'n't no better'n he had orter be. That's what
I says, says I."

To this general remark Dr. Small assented in his
invisible—shall I say *intangible?*—way.

"I allers think, maybe, that some folks has found
it best to leave home and go away. You can't
never tell. But when people is a-bein' robbed it's
well to look out. Hey?"

"I think so," said Small quietly, and, having
taken his hat and bowed a solemn and respectful
adieu, he departed.

He had not spoken twenty words, but he had
satisfied the news-monger of Flat Creek that Ralph
was a bad character at home and worthy of suspicion
of burglary.

CHAPTER XI

MISS MARTHA HAWKINS

"It's very good for the health to dig in the elements. I was quite emaciated last year at the East, and the doctor told me to dig in the elements. I got me a florial hoe and dug, and it's been most excellent for me."[1] Time, the Saturday following the Friday on which Ralph kept Shocky company as far as the "forks" near Granny Sanders's house. Scene, the Squire's garden. Ralph helping that worthy magistrate perform sundry little jobs such as a warm winter day suggests to the farmer. Miss Martha Hawkins, the Squire's niece, and his housekeeper in his present bereaved condition, leaning over the palings—pickets she called them—of the garden fence, talking to the master. Miss Hawkins was recently from Massachusetts. How many people there are in the most cultivated communities whose education is partial!

"It's very common for schoolmaster to dig in the elements at the East," proceeded Miss Martha. Like many other people born in the celestial empires (of which there are three—China, Virginia, Massachusetts), Miss Martha was not averse to

---

[1] Absurd as this speech seems, it is a literal transcript of words spoken in the author's presence by a woman who, like Miss Hawkins, was born in Massachusetts.

reminding outside barbarians of her good fortune in this regard. It did her good to speak of the East.

Now Ralph was amused with Miss Martha. She really had a good deal of intelligence despite her affectation, and conversation with her was both interesting and diverting. It helped him to forget Hannah, and Bud, and the robbery, and all the rest, and she was so delighted to find somebody to make an impression on that she had come out to talk while Ralph was at work. But just at this moment the schoolmaster was not so much interested in her interesting remarks, nor so much amused by her amusing remarks, as he should have been. He saw a man coming down the road riding one horse and leading another, and he recognized the horses at a distance. It must be Bud who was riding Means's bay mare and leading Bud's roan colt. Bud had been to mill, and as the man who owned the horse-mill kept but one old blind horse himself, it was necessary that Bud should take two. It required three horses to run the mill; the old blind one could have ground the grist, but the two others had to overcome the friction of the clumsy machine.

But it was not about the horse-mill that Ralph was thinking nor about the two horses. Since that Wednesday evening on which he escorted Hannah home from the spelling-school he had not seen Bud Means. If he had any lingering doubts of the truth of what Mirandy had said, they had been dissipated by the absence of Bud from school.

"When I was to Bosting——" Miss Martha was to Boston only once in her life, but as her visit to that sacred city was the most important occurrence of her life, she did not hesitate to air her reminiscences of it frequently. "When I was to Bosting," she was just saying, when, following the indication of Ralph's eyes, she saw Bud coming up the hill near Squire Hawkin's house. Bud looked red and sulky, and to Ralph's and Miss Martha Hawkins's polite recognitions he returned only a surly nod. They both saw that he was angry. Ralph was able to guess the meaning of his wrath.

Toward evening Ralph strolled through the Squire's cornfield toward the woods. The memory of the walk with Hannah was heavy upon the heart of the young master, and there was comfort in the very miserableness of the cornstalks with their disheveled blades hanging like tattered banners and rattling discordantly in the rising wind. Wandering without purpose, Ralph followed the rows of stalks first one way and then the other in a zigzag line, turning a right angle every minute or two. At last he came out in a woods mostly of beech, and he pleased his melancholy fancy by kicking the dry and silky leaves before him in billows, while the soughing of the wind through the long, vibrant boughs and slender twigs of the beech forest seemed to put the world into the wailing minor key of his own despair.

What a fascination there is in a path come upon suddenly without a knowledge of its termination! Here was one running in easy, irregular curves through the wood, now turning gently to the right in order to avoid a stump, now swaying suddenly to the left to gain an easier descent at a steep place, and now turning wantonly to the one side or the other, as if from very caprice in the man who by idle steps unconsciously marked the line of the foot-path at first. Ralph could not resist the impulse—who could?—to follow the path and find out its destination, and following it he came presently into a lonesome hollow, where a brook gurgled among the heaps of bare limestone rocks that filled its bed. Following the path still, he came upon a queer little cabin built of round logs, in the midst of a small garden-patch inclosed by a brush fence. The stick chimney, daubed with clay and topped with a barrel open at both ends, made this a typical cabin.

It flashed upon Ralph that this place must be Rocky Hollow, and that this was the house of old John Pearson, the one-legged basket-maker, and his rheumatic wife—the house that hospitably sheltered Shocky. Following his impulse, he knocked and was admitted, and was not a little surprised to find Miss Martha Hawkins there before him.

"You here, Miss Hawkins?" he said when he had returned Shocky's greeting and shaken hands with the old couple.

"Bless you, yes," said the old lady. "That blessed gyirl"—the old lady called her a girl by a sort of figure of speech perhaps—"that blessed gyirl's the kindest creetur you ever saw—comes here every day, most, to cheer a body up with somethin' or nuther."

Miss Martha blushed, and said "she came because Rocky Hollow looked so much like a place she used to know at the East. Mr. and Mrs. Pearson were the kindest people. They reminded her of people she knew at the East. When she was to Bosting——"

Here the old basket-maker lifted his head from his work, and said: "Pshaw! that talk about kyindness" (he was a Kentuckian and said *kyindness*) "is all humbug. I wonder so smart a woman as you don't know better. You come nearer to bein' kyind than anybody I know; but, laws a me! we're all selfish akordin' to my tell."

"You wasn't selfish when you set up with my father most every night for two weeks," said Shocky, as he handed the old man a splint.

"Yes, I was, too!" This in a tone that made Ralph tremble. "Your father was a miserable Britisher. I'd fit red-coats, in the war of eighteen-twelve, and lost my leg by one of 'em stickin' his dog-on'd bagonet right through it, that night at Lundy's Lane; but my messmate killed him though, which is a satisfaction to think on. And I didn't like your father 'cause he was a Britisher. But ef he'd a died right here in this free country, 'thout nobody to give him a drink of water, blamed ef I wouldn't a been ashamed to set on the platform at a Fourth of July barbecue, and to hold up my wooden leg fer to make the boys cheer! That was the selfishest thing I ever done. We're all selfish akordin' to my tell."

"You wasn't selfish when you took me that night, you know," and Shocky's face beamed with gratitude.

"Yes, I war, too, you little sass-box! What did I take you fer? Hey? Bekase I didn't like Pete Jones nor Bill Jones. They're thieves, dog-on 'em!"

Ralph shivered a little. The horse with the white forefoot and white nose galloped before his eyes again.

"They're a set of thieves. That's what they air."

"Please, Mr. Pearson, be careful, You'll get into trouble, you know, by talking that way," said Miss Hawkins. "You're just like a man that I knew at the East."

"Why, do you think an old soldier like me, hobbling on a wooden leg, is afraid of them thieves? Didn't I face the Britishers? Didn't I come home late last Wednesday night? I rather guess I must a took a little too much at Welch's grocery, and laid down in the middle of the street to rest. The boys thought 'twas funny to crate[1] me. I woke up kind o' cold, 'bout one in the mornin.' 'Bout two o'clock I come up Means's hill, and didn't I see Pete Jones, and them others that robbed the Dutchman, and somebody, I dunno who, a-crossin' the blue-grass paster to*wards* Jones's?' (Ralph

---

[1] When the first edition of this book appeared, the critic who analyzed the dialect in *The Nation* confessed that he did not know what to "crate" meant. It was a custom in the days of early Indiana barbarism for the youngsters of a village, on spying a sleeping drunkard, to hunt up a "queensware crate"—one of the cages of round withes in which crockery was shipped. This was turned upside down over the inebriate, and loaded with logs or any other heavy articles that would make escape difficult when the poor wretch should come to himself. It was a sort of rude punishment for inebriety, and it afforded a frog-killing delight to those who executed justice.

shivered.) "Don't shake your finger at me, old
woman. Tongue is all I've got to fight with now;
but I'll fight them thieves tell the sea goes dry, I
will. Shocky, gim me a splint."

"But you wasn't selfish when you tuck me."
Shocky stuck to his point most positively.

"Yes, I was, you little tow-headed fool! I didn't
take you kase I was good, not a bit of it. I hated
Bill Jones what keeps the poor-house, and I knowed
him and Pete would get you bound to some of
their click, and I didn't want no more thieves raised;
so when your mother hobbled, with you a-leadin'
her, poor blind thing! all the way over here on that
winter night, and said, 'Mr. Pearson, you're all the
friend I've got, and I want you to save my boy,'
why, you see I was selfish as ever I could be in
takin' of you. Your mother's cryin' sot me a-cryin'
too. We're all selfish in everything, akordin' to
my tell. Blamed ef we ha'n't, Miss Hawkins, only
sometimes I'd think you was real benev'lent ef I
didn't know we war all selfish."

CHAPTER XII

THE HARDSHELL PREACHER

"THEY's preachin' down to Bethel Meetin'-house to-day," said the Squire at breakfast. Twenty years in the West could not cure Squire Hawkins of saying "to" for "at". "I rather guess as how the old man Bosaw will give pertickeler fits to our folks to-day." For Squire Hawkins, having been expelled from the "Hardshell" church of which Mr. Bosaw was pastor, for the grave offense of joining a temperance society, had become a member of the "Reformers," the very respectable people who now call themselves "Disciples," but whom the profane will persist in calling "Campbellites." They had a church in the village of Clifty, three miles away.

I know that explanations are always abominable to story readers, as they are to story writers, but as so many of my readers have never had the inestimable privilege of sitting under the gospel as it is ministered in enlightened neighborhoods like Flat Creek, I find myself under the necessity—need-cessity the Rev. Mr. Bosaw would call it—of rising to explain. Some people think the "Hardshells" a myth, and some sensitive Baptist people at the East resent all allusion to them. But the "Hardshell Baptists," or, as they are otherwise called, the "Whisky Baptists," and the "Forty-gallon Baptists," exist in all the old Western and South-western States. They call themselves "Anti-means Baptists" from their Antinomian tenets. Their confession of faith is a caricature of Calvinism, and is expressed by their preachers about as follows: "Ef you're elected, you'll be saved; ef you a'n't, you'll be damned. God'll take keer of his elect. It's a sin to run Sunday-schools, or temp'rince s'cieties, or to send missionaries. You let God's business alone. What is to be will be, and you can't hender it." This writer has attended a Sunday-school, the superintendent of which was solemnly arraigned and expelled from the Hardshell Church for "meddling with God's business" by holding a Sunday-school. Of course the Hardshells are prodigiously illiterate, and often vicious. Some of their preachers are notorious drunkards. They sing their sermons out sometimes for three hours at a stretch.[1]

Ralph found that he was to ride the "clay-bank

---

[1] Even the Anti-means Baptists have suffered from the dire spirit of the age. They are to-day a very respectable body of people calling themselves "Primitive Baptists." Perhaps the description in the text never applied to the whole denomination, but only to the Hardshells of certain localities. Some of these intensely conservative churches, I have reason to believe, were always composed of reputable people. But what is said above is not in the least exaggerated as a description of many of the churches in Indiana and Illinois. Their opposition to the temperance reformation was both theoretical and practical. A rather able minister of the denomination whom I knew as a boy used to lie in besotted drunkenness by the roadside. I am sorry to confess that he once represented the county in the State legislature. The piece of a sermon given in this chapter was heard near Cairo, Illinois, in the days before the war. Most of the preachers were illiterate farmers. I have heard one of them hold forth two hours at a stretch. But even in that day there were men among the Hardshells whose ability and character commanded respect. This was true, especially in Kentucky, where able men like the two Dudleys held to the Antinomian wing of their denomination. But the Hardshells are perceptibly less hard than they were. You may march at the rear of the column among Hunkers and Hardshells if you will, but you are obliged to march. Those who will not go voluntarily, the time-spirit, walking behind, prods onward with a goad.

mare," the only one of the horses that would "carry double," and that consequently he would have to take Miss Hawkins behind him. If it had been Hannah instead, Ralph might not have objected to this "young Lochinvar" mode of riding with a lady on "the croup," but Martha Hawkins was another affair. He had only this consolation; his keeping the company of Miss Hawkins might serve to disarm the resentment of Bud. At all events, he had no choice. What designs the Squire had in this arrangement he could not tell; but the clay-bank mare carried him to meeting on that December morning, with Martha Hawkins behind. And as Miss Hawkins was not used to this mode of locomotion, she was in a state of delightful fright every time the horse sank to the knees in the soft, yellow Flat Creek clay.

"We don't go to church so at the East," she said. "The mud isn't so deep at the East. When I was to Bosting——" but Ralph never heard what happened when she was to Bosting, for just as she said Bosting the mare put her foot in a deep hole molded by the foot of the Squire's horse, and already full of muddy water.

As the mare's foot went twelve inches down into this track, the muddy water spurted higher than Miss Hawkins's head, and mottled her dress with golden spots of clay. She gave a little shriek, and declared that she had never "seen it so at the East."

The journey seemed a little long to Ralph, who found that the subjects upon which he and Miss Hawkins could converse were few; but Miss Martha was determined to keep things going, and once, when the conversation had died out entirely, she made a desperate effort to renew it by remarking as they met a man on horseback, "That horse switches his tail just as they do at the East. When I was to Bosting I saw horses switch their tails just that way."

What surprised Ralph was to see that Flat Creek went to meeting. Everybody was there—the Meanses, the Joneses, the Bantas, and all the rest. Everybody on Flat Creek seemed to be there, except the old wooden-legged basket-maker. His family was represented by Shocky, who had come, doubtless, to get a glimpse of Hannah, not to hear Mr. Bosaw preach. In fact, few were thinking of the religious service. They went to church as a common resort to hear the news, and to find out what was the current sensation.

On this particular morning there seemed to be some unusual excitement. Ralph perceived it as he rode up. An excited crowd, even though it be at a church-door on Sunday morning, can not conceal its agitation. Ralph deposited Miss Hawkins on the stile, and then got down himself, and paid her the closest attention to the door. This attention was for Bud's benefit. But Bud only stood with his hands in his pockets, scowling worse than ever. Ralph did not go in at the door. It was not the Flat Creek custom. The men gossiped outside, while the women chatted within. Whatever may have been the cause of the excitement, Ralph could not get at it. When he entered a little knot of people they became embarrassed, the group dissolved, and its component parts joined other companies. What had the current of conversation to do with him? He overheard Pete Jones saying that the blamed old wooden leg was in it anyhow. He'd been seen goin' home at two in the mornin'. And he could name somebody else ef he choosed. But it was best to clean out one at a time. And just then there was a murmur: "Meetin's took up." And the masculine element filled the empty half of the "hewed-log" church.

When Ralph saw Hannah looking utterly dejected, his heart smote him, and the great struggle set in again. Had it not been for the thought of the other battle, and the comforting presence of the Helper, I fear Bud's interests would have fared badly. But Ralph, with the spirit of a martyr, resolved to wait until he knew what the result of Bud's suit should be, and whether, indeed, the young Goliath had prior claims, as he evidently thought he had. He turned hopefully to the sermon, determined to pick up any crumbs of comfort that might fall from Mr. Bosaw's meager table.

In reporting a single specimen passage of Mr. Bosaw's sermon, I shall not take the liberty which Thucydides and other ancient historians did, of making the sermon and putting it into the hero's mouth, but shall give that which can be vouched for.

"You see, my respective hearers," he began—but alas! I can never picture to you the rich red nose, the see-sawing gestures, the nasal resonance, the sniffle, the melancholy minor key, and all that.

"My respective hearers-ah, you see-ah, as how-ah as my tex'-ah says that the ox-ah knoweth his owner-ah, and-ah the ass-ah his master's crib-ah. A-h-h! Now, my respective hearers-ah, they're a mighty sight of resemblance-ah atwext men-ah and oxen-ah." [Ralph could not help reflecting that there was a mighty sight of resemblance between some men and asses. But the preacher did not see this analogy. It lay too close to him], "bekase-ah, you see, men-ah is mighty like oxen-ah. Fer they's a tremengious defference-ah atwixt defferent oxen-ah, jest as thar is atwext defferent men-ah; fer the ox knoweth-ah his owner-ah, and the ass-ah, his master's crib-ah. Now, my respective hearers-ah" [the preacher's voice here grew mellow, and the succeeding sentences were in the most pathetic and lugubrious tones], "you all know-ah that your humble speaker-ah has got-ah jest the best yoke of steers-ah in this township-ah." [Here Betsey Short shook the floor with a suppressed titter.] "They a'n't no sech steers as them air two of mine-ah in this whole kedentry-ah. Them crack oxen over at Clifty-ah ha'n't a patchin' to mine-ah. Fer the ox knoweth his owner-ah, and the ass-ah his master's crib-ah.

"Now, my respective hearers-ah, they's a right smart sight of defference-ah atwext them air two oxen-ah, jest like they is atwext defferent men-ah. Fer-ah" [here the speaker grew earnest, and sawed the air, from this to the close, in a most frightful way], "fer-ah, you see-ah, when I go out-ah in the mornin'-ah to yoke-ah up-ah them air steers-ah, and I says-ah, 'Wo, Berry-ah! *Wo, Berry-ah!* Wo,

BERRY-AH', why Berry-ah jest stands stock still-ah and don't hardly breathe-ah while I put on the yoke-ah, and put in the bow-ah, and put in the key-ah, fer, my brethering-ah, and sistering-ah, the ox know-eth his owner-ah, and the ass-ah his master's crib-ah. Hal-le-lu-ger-ah!

"But-ah, my hearers-ah, but-ah when I stand at t'other eend of the yoke-ah and say, ' Come, Buck-ah! *Come, Buck-ah!* COME BUCK-AH! COME, BUCK-AH!' why what do you think-ah? Buck-ah, that ornery ole Buck-ah, 'stid of comin' right along-ah and puttin' his neck under-ah, acts jest like some men-ah what is fools-ah. Buck-ah jest kinder sorter stands off-ah, and kinder sorter puts his head down-ah this 'ere way-ah, and kinder looks mad-ah, and says, Boo-*oo-oo-OO-ah!*"

Alas! Hartsook found no spiritual edification there, and he was in no mood to be amused. And so, while the sermon drew on through two dreary hours, he forgot the preacher in noticing a bright green lizard which, having taken up its winter quarters behind the tin candlestick that hung just back of the preacher's head, had been deceived by the genial warmth coming from the great box-stove, and now ran out two or three feet from his shelter, looking down upon the red-nosed preacher in a most confidential and amusing manner. Sometimes he would retreat behind the candlestick, which was not twelve inches from the preacher's head, and then rush out again. At each reappearance Betsey Short would stuff her handkerchief into her mouth and shake in a most distressing way. Shocky wondered what the lizard was winking at the preacher about. And Miss Martha thought that it reminded her of a lizard that she see at the East, the time she was to Bosting, in a jar of alcohol in the Natural History Rooms. The Squire was not disappointed in his anticipation that Mr. Bosaw would attack his denomination with some fury. In fact, the old preacher outdid himself in his violent indignation at "these people that follow Campbell-ah, that thinks-ah that obejience-ah will save 'em-ah and that belongs-ah to temp'rince societies-ah and Sunday-schools-ah, and them air things-ah, that's not ortherized in the Bible-ah, but comes of the devil-ah, and takes folks as belongs to 'em to hell-ah."

As they came out the door Ralph rallied enough to remark: "He did attack your people, Squire."

"Oh, yes," said the Squire. "Didn't you see the Sarpent inspirin' him?"

But the long, long hours were ended and Ralph got on the clay-bank mare and rode up alongside the stile whence Miss Martha mounted. And as he went away with a heavy heart, he overheard Pete Jones call out to somebody:

"We'll tend to his case a Christmas." Christmas was two days off.

And Miss Martha remarked with much trepidation that poor Pearson would have to leave. She'd always been afraid that would be the end of it. It reminded her of something she heard at the East the time she was down to Bosting.

CHAPTER XIII

A STRUGGLE FOR THE MASTERY

THE school had closed on Monday evening as usual. The boys had been talking in knots all day. Nothing but the bulldog in the slender, resolute young master had kept down the rising storm. A teacher who has lost moral support at home, can not long govern a school. Ralph had effectually lost his popularity in the district, and the worst of it was that he could not divine from just what quarter the ill wind came, except that he felt sure of Small's agency in it somewhere. Even Hannah had slighted him, when he called at Means's on Monday morning to draw the pittance of pay that was due him.

He had expected a petition for a holiday on Christmas day. Such holidays are deducted from the teacher's time, and it is customary for the boys to "turn out" the teacher who refuses to grant them, by barring him out of the schoolhouse on Christmas and New Year's morning. Ralph had intended to grant a holiday if it should be asked, but it was not asked. Hank Banta was the ringleader in the disaffection, and he had managed to draw the surly Bud, who was present this morning, into it. It is but fair to say that Bud was in favor of making a request before resorting to extreme measures, but he was overruled. He gave it as his solemn opinion that the master was mighty peart, and they would be beat anyhow some way, but he would lick the master fer two cents ef he warn't so slim that he'd feel like he was fighting a baby.

And all that day things looked black. Ralph's countenance was cold and hard as stone, and Shocky trembled where he sat. Betsey Short tittered rather more than usual. A riot or a murder would have seemed amusing to her.

School was dismissed, and Ralph, instead of re-turning to the Squire's, set out for the village of Clifty, a few miles away. No one knew what he went for, and some suggested that he had "sloped."

But Bud said "he warn't that air kind. He was one of them air sort as died in their tracks, was Mr. Hartsook. They'd find him on the ground nex' morning, and he 'lowed the master war made of that air sort of stuff as would burn the dog-on'd ole schoolhouse to ashes, or blow it into splinters, but what he'd beat. Howsumdever he'd said he was a-goin' to help, and help he would; but all the sinno in Golier wouldn't be no account again the cute they was in the head of the master."

But Bud, discouraged as he was with the fear of Ralph's "cute", went like a martyr to the stake and took his place with the rest in the schoolhouse at nine o'clock at night. It may have been Ralph's intention to preoccupy the schoolhouse, for at ten o'clock Hank Banta was set shaking from head to foot at seeing a face that looked like the master's at the window. He waked up Bud and told him about it.

"Well, what are you a-tremblin' about, you coward?" growled Bud. "He won't shoot you; but he'll beat you at this game, I'll bet a hoss, and me, too, and make us both as 'shamed of ourselves as dogs with tin-kittles to their tails. You don't know the master, though he did duck you. But he'll larn you a good lesson this time, and me too, like as not." And Bud soon snored again, but Hank shook with fear every time he looked at the blackness outside the windows. He was sure he heard footfalls. He would have given anything to have been at home.

When morning came, the pupils began to gather early. A few boys who were likely to prove of service in the coming siege were admitted through the window, and then everything was made fast, and a "snack" was eaten.

"How do you 'low he'll get in?" said Hank, trying to hide his fear.

"How do I 'low?" said Bud. "I don't 'low nothin' about it. You might as well ax me where I 'low the nex' shootin' star is a-goin' to drap. Mr. Hartsook's mighty onsartin. But he'll git in, though, and tan your hide fer you, you see ef he don't. *Ef* he don't blow up the schoolhouse with gunpowder!" This last was thrown in by way of alleviating the fears of the cowardly Hank, for whom Bud had a great contempt.

The time for school had almost come. The boys inside were demoralized by waiting. They began to hope that the master had "sloped." They dreaded to see him coming.

"I don't believe he'll come," said Hank, with a cold shiver. "It's past school-time."

"Yes, he will come, too," said Bud. "And he 'lows to come in here mighty quick. I don't know how. But he'll be a-standin' at that air desk when it's nine o'clock. I'll bet a thousand dollars on that. *Ef* he don't take it into his head to blow us up!" Hank was now white.

Some of the parents came along, accidentally of course, and stopped to see the fun, sure that Bud would thrash the master if he tried to break in. Small, on the way to see a patient perhaps, reined up in front of the door. Still no Ralph. It was just five minutes before nine. A rumor now gained currency that he had been seen going to Clifty the evening before, and that he had not come back though in fact Ralph had come back, and had slept at Squire Hawkins's.

"There's the master," cried Betsey Short, who stood out in the road shivering and giggling alternately. For Ralph at that moment emerged from the sugar-camp by the schoolhouse, carrying a board.

"Ho! ho!" laughed Hank, "he thinks he'll smoke us out. I guess he'll find us ready." The boys had let the fire burn down, and there was now nothing but hot hickory coals on the hearth.

"I tell you he'll come in. He didn't go to Clifty fer nothin'," said Bud, who sat still on one of the benches which leaned against the door. "I don't know how, but they's lots of ways of killing a cat besides chokin' her with butter. He'll come in— *ef* he don't blow us all sky-high!"

Ralph's voice was now heard, demanding that the door be opened.

"Let's open her," said Hank, turning livid with fear at the firm, confident tone of the master.

Bud straightened himself up. "Hank, you're a coward. I've got a mind to kick you. You got me into this blamed mess, and now you want to craw-fish. You jest tech one of these 'ere fastenin's, and I'll lay you out flat of your back afore you can say Jack Robinson."

The teacher was climbing to the roof with the board in hand.

"That air won't win," laughed Pete Jones outside. He saw that there was no smoke. Even Bud began to hope that Ralph would fail for once. The master was now on the ridge-pole of the school-house. He took a paper from his pocket, and deliberately poured the contents down the chimney.

Mr. Pete Jones shouted "Gunpowder!" and set off down the road to be out of the way of the explosion. Dr. Small remembered, probably, that his patient might die while he sat there, and started on.

But Ralph emptied the paper, and laid the board over the chimney. What a row there was inside! The benches that were braced against the door were thrown down, and Hank Banta rushed out, rubbing his eyes, coughing frantically, and sure that he had been blown up. All the rest followed, Bud bringing up the rear sulkily, but coughing and sneezing for dear life. Such a smell of sulphur as came from that schoolhouse.

Betsey had to lean against the fence to giggle.

As soon as all were out, Ralph threw the board off the chimney, leaped to the ground, entered the schoolhouse, and opened the windows. The school soon followed him, and all was still.

"Would he thrash?" This was the important question in Hank Banta's mind. And the rest looked for a battle with Bud.

"It is just nine o'clock," said Ralph, consulting his watch, "and I'm glad to see you all here promptly. I should have given you a holiday if you had asked me like gentlemen yesterday. On the whole, I think I shall give you a holiday, anyhow. The school is dismissed."

And Hank felt foolish.

And Bud secretly resolved to thrash Hank or the master, he didn't care which.

And Mirandy looked the love she could not utter.

And Betsey giggled.

CHAPTER XIV

A CRISIS WITH BUD

RALPH sat still at his desk. The school had gone. All at once he became conscious that Shocky sat yet in his accustomed place upon the hard, backless bench.

"Why, Shocky, haven't you gone yet?"

"No—sir—I was waitin' to see if you warn't a-goin', too—I——"

"Well?"

"I thought it would make me feel as if God warn't quite so fur away to talk to you. It did the other day."

The master rose and put his hand on Shocky's head. Was it the brotherhood in affliction that made Shocky's words choke him so? Or, was it the weird thoughts that he expressed? Or, was it the recollection that Shocky was Hannah's brother? Hannah, so far, far away from him now! At any rate, Shocky, looking up for the smile on which he fed, saw the relaxing of the master's face, that had been as hard as stone, and felt just one hot tear on his hand.

"P'r'aps God's forgot you, too," said Shocky in a sort of half soliloquy. "Better get away from Flat Creek. You see God forgets everybody down here. 'Cause 'most everybody forgets God, 'cept

Mr. Bosaw, and I 'low God don't no ways keer to be remembered by sich as him. Leastways I wouldn't if I was God, you know. I wonder what becomes of folks when God forgets 'em?" And Shocky, seeing that the master had resumed his seat and was looking absently into the fire, moved slowly out the door.

"Shocky!" called the master.

The little poet came back and stood before him.

"Shocky, you mustn't think God has forgotten you. God brings things out right at last." But Ralph's own faith was weak, and his words sounded hollow and hypocritical to himself. Would God indeed bring things out right?

He sat musing a good while, trying to convince himself of the truth of what he had just been saying to Shocky—that God would indeed bring things out right at last. Would it all come out right if Bud married Hannah? Would it all come out right if he were driven from Flat Creek with a dark suspicion upon his character? Did God concern Himself with these things? Was there any God? It was the same old struggle between Doubt and Faith. And when Ralph looked up, Shocky had departed.

In the next hour Ralph fought the old battle of Armageddon. I shall not describe it. You will fight it in your own way. No two alike. The important thing is the End. If you come out as he did, with the doubt gone and the trust in God victorious, it matters little just what shape the battle may take. Since Jacob became Israel there have never been two such struggles alike, save in that they all end either in victory or in defeat.

It was after twelve o'clock on that Christmas day when Ralph put his head out the door of the school-house and called out: "Bud, I'd like to see you."

Bud did not care to see the master, for he had inly resolved to "thrash him" and have done with him. But he couldn't back out, certainly not in sight of the others who were passing along the road with him.

"I don't want the rest of you," said Ralph in a decided way, as he saw that Hank and one or two others were resolved to come also.

"Thought maybe you'd want somebody to see far play," said Hank as he went off sheepishly.

"If I did, you would be the last one I should ask," said Ralph. "There's no unfair play in Bud, and there is in you." And he shut the door.

"Now, looky here, Mr. Ralph Hartsook," said Bud. "You don't come no gum games over me with your saft sodder and all that. I've made up my mind. You've got to promise to leave these 'ere diggins, or I've got to thrash you."

"You'll have to thrash me, then," said Ralph, turning a little pale, but remembering the bulldog. "But you'll tell me what it's all about, won't you?"

"You know well enough. Folks says you know more 'bout the robbery at the Dutchman's than you orter. But I don't believe them. Fer them as says it is liars and thieves theirselves. 'Ta'n't fer none of that. And I shan't tell you what it *is* fer. So now, if you won't travel, why, take off your coat and git ready fer a thrashing."

The master took off his coat and showed his slender arms. Bud laid his off, and showed the physique of a prize-fighter.

"You a'n't a-goin to fight *me?*" said Bud.

"Not unless you make me."

"Why I could chaw you all up."

"I know that."

"Well, you're the grittiest feller I ever did see, and ef you'd jest kep off of my ground I wouldn't a touched you. But I a'n't a-goin' to be cut out by no feller a livin' 'thout thrashin' him in an inch of his life. You see I wanted to git out of this Flat Crick way. We're a low-lived set here in Flat Crick. And I says to myself, I'll try to be somethin' more nor Pete Jones, and dad, and these other triflin', good-fer-nothin' ones 'bout here. And when you come I says, There's one as'll help me. And what do you do with yor book-larnin' and town manners but start right out to git away the gal that I'd picked out, when I'd picked her out kase I thought, not bein' Flat Crick born herself, she might help a feller to do better! Now I won't let nobody cut me out without givin' 'em the best thrashin' it's in these 'ere arms to give."

"But I haven't tried to cut you out."

"You can't fool *me.*"

"Bud, listen to me, and then thrash me if you will. I went with that girl once. When I found you had some claims, I gave her up. Not because I was afraid of you, for I would rather have taken the worst thrashing you can give me than give her up. But I haven't spoken to her since the night of the first spelling-school."

"You lie!" said Bud, doubling his fists.

Ralph grew red.

"You was a-waitin' on her last Sunday right afore my eyes, and a-tryin' to ketch my attention too. So when you're ready say so."

"Bud, there is some misunderstanding." Hartsook spoke slowly and felt bewildered. "I tell you that I did not speak to Hannah last Sunday, and you know I didn't."

"Hanner!" Bud's eyes grew large. "Hanner!" Here he gasped for breath, and looked around, "Hanner!" He couldn't get any further than the name at first. "Why, plague take it, who said Hanner?"

"Mirandy said you were courting Hannah," said Ralph, feeling round in a vague way to get his ideas together.

"Mirandy! Thunder! You believed Mirandy! Well! Now, looky here, Mr. Hartsook, ef you was to say that my sister lied, I'd lick you till yer hide wouldn't hold shucks. But *I* say, a-twix you and me and the gate-post, don't you never believe nothing that Mirandy Means says. Her and marm has set theirselves like fools to git you. Hanner! Well, she's a mighty nice gal, but you're welcome to *her.* I never tuck no shine that air way. But I was out of school last Thursday and Friday a-shucking corn to take to mill a-Saturday. And when I come past the Squire's and seed you talking to a gal as is a gal, you know"—here Bud hesitated and looked foolish—"I felt hoppin' mad."

Bud put on his coat.

Ralph put on his coat.

Then they shook hands and Bud went out. Ralph sat looking into the fire. There was no conscientious difficulty now in the way of his claiming Hannah. The dry forestick lying on the rude stone andirons burst into a blaze. The smoldering hope in the heart of Ralph Hartsook did the same. He could have Hannah if he could win her. But there came slowly back the recollection of his lost standing in Flat Creek. There was circumstantial evidence against him. It was evident that Hannah believed something of this. What other stories Small might have put in circulation he did not know. Would Small try to win Hannah's love to throw it away again, as he had done with others? At least he would not spare any pains to turn the heart of the bound girl against Ralph.

The bright flame on the forestick, which Ralph had been watching, flickered and burned low.

CHAPTER XV

THE CHURCH OF THE BEST LICKS

JUST as the flame on the forestick, which Ralph had watched so intensely, flickered and burned low, and just as Ralph with a heavy but not quite hopeless heart rose to leave, the latch lifted and Bud reentered.

"I wanted to say something," he stammered, "but you know it's hard to say it. I ha'n't no book-larnin' to speak of, and some things is hard to say when a man ha'n't got book-words to say 'em with. And they's some things a man can't hardly ever say anyhow to anybody."

Here Bud stopped. But Ralph spoke in such a matter-of-course way in reply that he felt encouraged to go on.

"You gin up Hanner kase you thought she belonged to me. That's more'n I'd a done by a long shot. Now, arter I left here jest now, I says to myself, a man what can gin up his gal on account of sech a feeling fer the rights of a Flat Cricker like me, why, dog-on it, says I, sech a man is the man as can help me do better. I don't know whether you're a Hardshell or a Saftshell, or a Methodist, or a Campbellite, or a New Light, or a United Brother, or a Millerite, or what-not. But I says, the man what can do the clean things by a ugly feller like me, and stick to it, when I was jest ready to eat him up, is a kind of a man to tie to."

Here Bud stopped in fright at his own volubility, for he had run his words off like a piece learned by heart, as though afraid that if he stopped he would not have courage to go on.

Ralph said that he did not belong to any church, and he was afraid he couldn't do Bud much good. But his tone was full of sympathy, and, what is better than sympathy, a yearning for sympathy

"You see," said Bud, "I wanted to git out of this low-lived, Flat Crick way of livin'. We're a hard set down here, Mr. Hartsook. And I'm gittin' to be one of the hardest of 'em. But I never could git no good out of Bosaw with his whisky and meanness. And I went to the Mount Tabor church concert. I heard a man discussin' baptism, and regeneration, and so on. That didn't seem no cure for me, I went to a revival over at Clifty. Well, 'twarn't no use. First night they was a man that spoke about Jesus Christ in sech a way that I wanted to foller him everywhere. But I didn't feel fit. Next night I come back with my mind made up that I'd try Jesus Christ, and see ef he'd have me. But laws! they was a big man that night that preached hell. Not that I don't believe they's a hell. They's plenty not a thousand miles away as deserves it, and I don't know as I'm too good for it myself. But he pitched it at us, and stuck it in our faces in sech a way that I got mad. And I says, Well, ef God sends me to hell he can't make me holler 'nough nohow. You see my dander was up. And when my dander's up, I wouldn't gin up fer the devil his-self. The preacher was so insultin' with his way of doin' it. He seemed to be kind of glad that we was to be damned, and he preached somethin' like some folks swears. It didn't sound a bit like the Christ the little man preached about the night afore. So what does me and a lot of fellers do but slip out and cut off the big preacher's stirrups, and hang 'em on to the rider of the fence, and then set his hoss loose! And from that day, sometimes I did, and sometimes I didn't, want to be better. And to-day it seemed to me that you must know some-thin' as would help me."

Nothing is worse than a religious experience kept ready to be exposed to the gaze of everybody, whether the time is appropriate or not. But never was a religious experience more appropriate than the account which Ralph gave to Bud of his Strug-gle in the Dark. The confession of his weakness and wicked selfishness was a great comfort to Bud.

"Do you think that Jesus Christ would—would —well, do you think He'd help a poor, unlarnt Flat Cricker like me?"

"I think He was a sort of a Flat Creeker Him-self," said Ralph, slowly and very earnestly.

"You don't say?" said Bud, almost getting off his seat.

"Why, you see the town He lived in was a rough place. It was called Nazareth, which meant 'Bushtown.'"

"You don't say?"

"And He was called a Nazarene, which was about the same as 'backwoodsman.'"

And Ralph read the different passages which he had studied at Sunday-school, illustrating the condescension of Jesus, the stories of the publicans, the harlots, the poor, who came to Him. And he read about Nathanael, who lived only six miles away, saying, 'Can any good thing come out of Nazareth?'"

"Jus' what Clifty folks says about Flat Crick," broke in Bud.

"Do you think I could begin without being baptized?" he added presently.

"Why not? Let's begin now to do the best we can, by His help."

"You mean, then, that I'm to begin now to put in my best licks for Jesus Christ, and that He'll help me?"

This shocked Ralph's veneration a little. But it was the sincere utterance of an earnest soul. It may not have been an orthodox start, but it was the one start for Bud. And there be those who have repeated with the finest æsthetic appreciation the old English liturgies who have never known religious aspiration so sincere as that of this ignorant young Hercules, whose best confession was that he meant hereafter "to put in his best licks for Jesus Christ." And there be those who can define repentance and faith to the turning of a hair who never made so genuine a start for the kingdom of Heaven as Bud Means did.

Ralph said yes, that he thought that was just it. At least, he guessed if there was something more, the man that was putting in his best licks would be sure to find it out.

"Do you think He'd help a feller? Seems to me it would be number one to have God help you. Not to help you fight other folks, but to help you when it comes to fighting the devil inside. But you see I don't belong to no church."

"Well, let's you and me have one right off. Two people that help one another to serve God make a church."

I am afraid this ecclesiastical theory will not be considered orthodox. It was Ralph's, and I write it down at the risk of bringing him into condemnation.

But other people before the days of Bud and Ralph have discussed church organization when they should have been doing Christian work. For both of them had forgotten the danger that hung over the old basket-maker, until Shocky burst into the schoolhouse, weeping. Indeed, the poor, nervous little frame was ready to go into convulsions.

"Miss Hawkins——"

Bud started at mention of the name.

"Miss Hawkins has just been over to say that a crowd is going to tar and feather Mr. Pearson to-night. And——" here Shocky wept again. "And he won't run, but he's took up the old flintlock, and says he'll die in his tracks."

CHAPTER XVI

THE CHURCH MILITANT

BUD was doubly enlisted on the side of John Pearson, the basket-maker. In the first place, he knew that this persecution of the unpopular old man was only a blind to save somebody else; that they were thieves who cried, "Stop thief!" And he felt consequently that this was a chance to put his newly-formed resolutions into practice. The Old Testament religious life, which consists in fighting the Lord's enemies, suited Bud's temper and education. It might lead to something better. It was the best possible to him, now. But I am afraid I shall have to acknowledge that there was a second motive that moved Bud to this championship. The good heart of Martha Hawkins having espoused the cause of the basket-maker, the heart of Bud Means could not help feeling warmly on the same side. Blessed is that man in whose life the driving of duty and the drawing of love impel the same way! But why speak of the driving of duty? For already Bud was learning the better lesson of serving God for the love of God.

The old basket-maker was the most unpopular man in Flat Creek district. He had two great vices. He would go to Clifty and have a "spree" once in three months. And he would tell the truth in a most unscrupulous manner. A man given to plain speaking was quite as objectionable in Flat Creek as he would have been in France under the Empire, the Commune, or the Republic, and almost as objectionable as he would be in any refined community in America. People who live in glass houses have a horror of people who throw stones. And the old basket-maker, having no friends, was a good scapegoat. In driving him off, Pete Jones would get rid of a dangerous neighbor and divert attention from himself. The immediate crime of the basket-maker was that he had happened to see too much.

"Mr. Hartsook," said Bud, when they got out into the road, "you'd better go straight home to the Squire's. Bekase ef this lightnin' strikes a second time it'll strike awful closte to you. You hadn't better be seen with us. Which way did you come, Shocky?"

"Why, I tried to come down the holler, but I met Jones right by the big road, and he sweared at me and said he'd kill me ef I didn't go back and stay. And so I went back to the house and then slipped out through the graveyard. You see I was bound to come ef I got skinned. For Mr. Pearson's stuck to me and I mean to stick to him, you see."

Bud led Shocky through the graveyard. But when they reached the forest path from the graveyard he thought that perhaps it was not best to "show his hand," as he expressed it, too soon.

"Now, Shocky," he said, "do you run ahead and tell the ole man that I want to see him right off down by the Spring-in-rock. I'll keep closte behind you, and ef anybody offers to trouble you, do you let off a yell and I'll be thar in no time."

When Ralph left the schoolhouse he felt mean. There were Bud and Shocky gone on an errand of mercy, and he, the truant member of the Church of the Best Licks, was not with them. The more he thought of it the more he seemed to be a coward, and the more he despised himself; so, yielding as usual to the first brave impulse, he leaped nimbly over the fence and started briskly through the forest in a direction intersecting the path on which were Bud and Shocky. He came in sight just in time to see the first conflict of the Church in the Wilderness with her foes.

For Shocky's little feet went more swiftly on their eager errand than Bud had anticipated He got farther out of Bud's reach than the latter intended he should, and he did not discover Pete Jones until Pete, with his hog-drover's whip was right upon him.

Shocky tried to halloo for Bud, but he was like one in a nightmare. The yell died into a whisper which could not have been heard ten feet.

I shall not repeat Mr. Jones' words. They were frightfully profane. But he did not stop at words. He swept his whip round and gave little Shocky one terrible cut. Then the voice was released, and the piercing cry of pain brought Bud down the path flying.

"You good-for-nothing scoundrel," growled Bud, "you're a coward and a thief to be a-beatin' a little creetur like him!" and with that Bud walked up on Jones, who prudently changed position in such a way as to get the upper side of the hill.

"Well, I'll gin you the upper side, but come on," cried Bud, "ef you a'n't afeared to fight somebody besides a poor little sickly baby or a crippled soldier. Come on!"

Pete was no insignificant antagonist. He had been a great fighter, and his well-seasoned arms were like iron. He had not the splendid set of Bud, but he had more skill and experience in the rude tournament of fists to which the backwoods is so much given. Now, being out of sight of witnesses and sure that he could lie about the fight afterward, he did not scruple to take advantages which would have disgraced him forever if he had taken them in a public fight on election day or at a muster. He took the uphill side, and he clubbed his whip-stalk, striking Bud with all his force with the heavy end, which, coward-like, he had loaded with lead. Bud threw up his strong left arm and parried the blow, which, however, was so fierce that it fractured one of the bones of the arm. Throwing away his whip Pete rushed upon Bud furiously, intending to overpower him, but Bud slipped quickly to one side and let Jones pass down the hill, and as Jones came up again Means dealt him one crushing blow that sent him full length upon the ground. Nothing but the leaves saved him from a most terrible fall. Jones sprang to his feet more angry than ever at being whipped by one whom he regarded as a boy, and drew a long dirk-knife. But he was blind with rage, and Bud dodged the knife, and this time gave Pete a blow on the nose which marred the homeliness of that feature and doubled the fellow up against a tree ten feet away.

Ralph came in sight in time to see the beginning of the fight, and he arrived on the ground just as Pete Jones went down under the well-dealt blow from the only remaining fist of Bud Means.

While Ralph examined Bud's disabled left arm Pete picked himself up slowly, and, muttering that he felt "consid'able shuck up like," crawled away like a whipped puppy. To every one whom he met, Pete, whose intellect seemed to have weakened in sympathy with his frame, remarked feebly that he was consid'able shuck up like, and vouchsafed no other explanation. Even to his wife he only said that he felt purty consid'able shuck up like, and that the boys would have to get on to-night without him. There are some scoundrels whose very malignity is shaken out of them for the time being by a thorough drubbing.

"I'm afraid you're going to have trouble with your arm, Bud," said Ralph tenderly.

"Never mind; I put in my best licks fer *Him*, that air time, Mr. Hartsook." Ralph shivered a little at thought of this, but if it was right to knock Jones down at all, why might not Bud do it "heartily as unto the Lord?"

Gideon did not feel any more honest pleasure in chastising the Midianites than did Bud in sending Pete Jones away purty consid'able shuck up like.

CHAPTER XVII

A COUNCIL OF WAR

SHOCKY, whose feet had flown as soon as he saw the final fall of Pete Jones, told the whole story to the wondering and admiring ears of Miss Hawkins, who unhappily could not remember anything at the East just like it; to the frightened ears of the rheumatic old lady who felt sure her ole man's talk and stubbornness would be the ruin of him, and to the indignant ears of the old soldier who was hobbling up and down, sentinel-wise, in front of his cabin, standing guard over himself.

"No, I won't leave," he said to Ralph and Bud. "You see I jest won't. What would Gin'ral Winfield Scott say ef he knew that one of them as fit at Lundy's Lane backed out, retreated, run fer fear of a passel of thieves? No, sir; me and the old flintlock will live and die together. I'll put a thunderin' charge of buckshot into the first one of them scoundrels as comes up the holler. It'll be another Lundy's Lane. And you, Mr. Hartsook, may send Scott word that ole Pearson, as fit at Lundy's Lane under him, died a-fightin' thieves on Rocky Branch, in Hoopole Kyounty, State of Injeanny."

And the old man hobbled faster and faster, taxing his wooden leg to the very utmost, as if his victory depended on the vehemence with which he walked his beat.

Mrs. Pearson sat wringing her hands and looking appealingly at Martha Hawkins, who stood in the door, in despair, looking appealingly at Bud. Bud was stupefied by the old man's stubbornness and his own pain, and in his turn appealed mutely to the master, in whose resources he had boundless confidence. Ralph, seeing that all depended on him, was taxing his wits to think of some way to get round Pearson's stubbornness. Shocky hung to the old man's coat and pulled away at him with many entreating words, but the venerable, bareheaded, sentinel strode up and down furiously, with his flintlock on his shoulder and his basket-knife in his belt.

Just at this point somebody could be seen indistinctly through the bushes coming up the hollow.

"Halt!" cried the old hero. "Who goes there?"

"It's me, Mr. Pearson. Don't shoot me, please."

It was the voice of Hannah Thomson. Hearing that the whole neighborhood was rising against the benefactor of Shocky and of her family, she had slipped away from the eyes of her mistress, and run with breathless haste to give warning in the cabin on Rocky Branch. Seeing Ralph, she blushed, and went into the cabin.

"Well," said Ralph, "the enemy is not coming yet. Let us hold a council of war.'

This thought came to Ralph like an inspiration. It pleased the old man's whim, and he sat down on the door-step.

"Now, I suppose," said Ralph, "that General Winfield Scott always looked into things a little before he went into a fight. Didn't he?"

"*To* be sure," assented the old man.

"Well," said Ralph. "What is the condition of the enemy? I suppose the whole neighborhood's against us."

"*To* be sure," said the old man. The rest were silent, but all felt the statement to be about true.

"Next," said Ralph, "I suppose General Winfield Scott would always inquire into the condition of his own troops. Now let us see. Captain Pearson has Bud, who is the right wing, badly crippled by having his arm broken in the first battle." (Miss Hawkins looked pale.)

"*To* be sure," said the old man.

"And I am the left wing, pretty good at giving advice, but very slender in a fight."

"*To* be sure," said the old man.

"And Shocky and Miss Martha and Hannah good aids, but nothing in a battle."

"*To* be sure," said the basket-maker, a little doubtfully.

"Now let's look at the arms and accouterments, I think you call them. Well, this old musket has been loaded——"

"This ten year," said the old lady.

"And the lock is so rusty that you could not cock it when you wanted to take aim at Hannah."

The old man looked foolish, and muttered "*To* be sure."

"And there isn't another round of ammunition in the house."

The old man was silent.

"Now let us look at the incumbrances. Here's

the old lady and Shocky. If you fight, the enemy will be pleased. It will give them a chance to kill you. And then the old lady will die and they will do with Shocky as they please."

"*To* be sure," said the old man reflectively.

"Now," said Ralph, "General Winfield Scott, under such circumstances, would retreat in good order. Then, when he could muster his forces rightly, he would drive the enemy from his ground."

"To be sure," said the old man. "What ort I to do?"

"Have you any friends?"

"Well, yes; ther's my brother over in Jackson Kyounty. I mout go there."

"Well," said Bud, "do you just go down to Spring-in-rock and stay there. Them folks won't be here tell midnight. I'll come fer you at nine with my roan colt, and I'll set you down over on the big road on Buckeye Run. Then you can git on the mail-wagon that passes there about five o-clock in the mornin', and go over to Jackson County and keep shady till we want you to face the enemy and to swear agin some folks. And then we'll send fer you."

"To be sure," said the old man in a broken voice. "I reckon General Winfield Scott wouldn't disapprove of such a maneuver as that thar."

Miss Martha beamed on Bud to his evident delight, for he carried his painful arm part of the way home with her. Ralph noticed that Hannah looked at *him* with a look full of contending emotions. He read admiration, gratitude, and doubt in the expression of her face, as she turned toward home.

"Well, good-by, ole woman," said Pearson, as he took up his little handkerchief full of things and started for his hiding-place; "good-by. I didn't never think I'd desart you, and ef the old flintlock hadn't a been rusty, I'd a staid and died right here by the ole cabin. But I reckon 'ta'n't best to be brash."[1]   And Shocky looked after him, as he hobbled away over the stones, more than ever convinced that God had forgotten all about things on Flat Creek.   He gravely expressed his opinion to the master the next day.

---

[1] The elaborate etymological treatment of this word in its various forms in our best dictionary is a fine illustration of the fact that something more than scholarship is needed for penetrating the mysteries of current folk-speech. *Brash*—often *bresh*—in the sense of refuse boughs of trees, is only another form of *brush;* the two are used as one word by the people. *Brash* in the sense of brittle has no conscious connection with the noun in popular usage, but it is accounted by the people the same word as *brash* in the sense of rash or impetuous. The suggestion in the Century Dictionary that the words spelled *brash* are of modern formation violates the soundest canon of antiquarian research, which is that a word phrase or custom widely diffused among plain or rustic people is of necessity of ancient origin. Now *brash*, the adjective, exists in both senses in two or three of the most widely separated dialects of the United States, and hence must have come from England. Indeed, it appears in Wright's Dictionary of Provincial English in precisely the sense it has in the text.

CHAPTER XVIII

ODDS AND ENDS

THE Spring-in-rock, or, as it was sometimes, by a curious perversion, called, the "rock-in-spring," was a spring running out of a cave-like fissure in a high limestone cliff. Here the old man sheltered himself on that dreary Christmas evening, until Bud brought his roan colt to the top of the cliff above, and he and Ralph helped the old man up the cliff and into the saddle. Ralph went back to bed, but Bud, who was only too eager to put in his best licks, walked by the side of old John Pearson the six miles over to Buckeye Run, and at last, after eleven o'clock, he deposited him in a hollow sycamore by the road, there to wait the coming of the mail-wagon that would carry him into Jackson County.

"Good-by," said the basket-maker, as Bud mounted the colt to return. "Ef I'm wanted jest send me word, and I'll make a forrard movement any time. I don't like this 'ere thing of running off in the night-time. But I reckon General Winfield Scott would a ordered a retreat ef he'd a been in my shoes. I'm lots obleeged to you. Akordin' to my tell, we're all of us selfish in everything; but I'll be dog-on'd ef I don't believe you and one or two more is exceptions."

Whether it was that the fact that Pete Jones had

got consid'able shuck up demoralized his followers, or whether it was that the old man's flight was suspected, the mob did not turn out in very great force, and the tarring was postponed indefinitely, for by the time they came together it became known somehow that the man with a wooden leg had outrun them all. But the escape of one devoted victim did not mollify the feelings of the people toward the next one.

By the time Bud returned his arm was very painful, and the next day he went under Dr. Small's treatment to reduce the fracture. Whatever suspicions Bud might have of Pete Jones, he was not afflicted with Ralph's dread of the silent young doctor. And if there was anything Small admired it was physical strength and courage. Small wanted Bud on his side, and least of all did he want him to be Ralph's champion. So that the silent, cool, and skillful doctor went to work to make an impression on Bud Means.

Other influences were at work upon him also. Mrs. Means volleyed and thundered in her usual style about his "takin' up with a one-legged thief, and runnin' arter that master that was a mighty suspicious kind of a customer, akordin' to her tell. She'd allers said so. Ef she'd a been consulted he wouldn't a been hired. He warn't fit company fer nobody."

And old Jack Means 'lowed Bud must want to have *their* barns burnt like some other folkses had been. Fer his part, he had sense enough to know they was some people as it wouldn't do to set a body's self agin. And as fer him, he didn't butt his brains out agin a buckeye-tree. Not when he was sober. And so they managed, during Bud's confinement to the house, to keep him well supplied with all the ordinary discomforts of life.

But one visit from Martha Hawkins, ten words of kindly inquiry from her, and the remark that his broken arm reminded her of something she had seen at the East and something somebody said the time she was to Bosting, were enough to repay the champion a thousand fold for all that he suffered. Indeed, that visit, and the recollection of Ralph's saying that Jesus Christ was a sort of a Flat Creeker himself, were manna in the wilderness to Bud.

Poor Shocky was sick. The excitement had been too much for him, and though his fever was very slight it was enough to produce just a little delirium. Either Ralph or Miss Martha was generally at the cabin.

"They're coming," said Shocky to Ralph, "they're coming. Pete Jones is a-going to bind me out for a hundred years. I wish Hanner would hold me so's he couldn't. God's forgot all about us here in Flat Creek, and there's nobody to help it."

And he shivered at every sudden sound. He was never free from this delirious fright except when the master held him tight in his arms. He staggered around the floor, the very shadow of Shocky, and was so terrified by the approach of darkness that Ralph staid in the cabin on Wednesday night and Miss Hawkins staid on Thursday night. On Friday, Bud sent a note to Ralph, asking him to come and see him.

"You see, Mr. Hartsook, I ha'n't forgot what we said about puttin' in our best licks for Jesus Christ. I've been a-trying to read some about Him while I set here. And I read where he said something about doing fer the least of His brethren being all the same like as if it was done fer Jesus Christ His-self. Now there's Shocky. I reckon, p'r'aps, ef anybody is a little brother of Jesus Christ, it is that Shocky. Pete Jones and his brother Bill is detar-mined to have him back there to-morry. Bekase, you see, Pete's one of the County Commissioners, and to-morry's the day that they bind out. He wants to bind out that boy jes' to spite ole Pearson and you and me. You see, the ole woman's been helped by the neighbors, and he'll claim Shocky to be a pauper, and they a'n't no human soul here as dares to do a thing contrary to Pete. Couldn't you git him over to Lewisburg? I'll lend you my roan colt."

Ralph thought a minute. He dared not take Shocky to the uncle's where he found his only home. But there was Miss Nancy Sawyer, the old maid who was everybody's blessing. He could ask her to keep him. And, at any rate, he would save Shocky somehow.

As he went out in the dusk, he met Hannah in the lane.

CHAPTER XIX

FACE TO FACE

In the lane, in the dark, under the shadow of the barn, Ralph met Hannah carrying her bucket of milk (they have no pails in Indiana).[1] He could see only the white foam on the milk, and Hannah's white face. Perhaps it was well that he could not see how white Hannah's face was at that moment when a sudden trembling made her set down the heavy bucket. At first neither spoke. The recollection of all the joy of that walk together in the night came upon them both. And a great sense of loss made the night seem supernaturally dark to Ralph. Nor was it any lighter in the hopeless heart of the bound girl. The presence of Ralph did not now, as before, make the darkness of her life light.

"Hannah——" said Ralph presently, and stopped. For he could not finish the sentence. With a rush there came upon him a consciousness of the suspicions that filled Hannah's mind. And with it there came a feeling of guilt. He saw himself from her stand-point, and felt a remorse almost as keen as it

---

[1] The total absence of the word *pail* not only from the dialect, but even from cultivated speech in the Southern and Border States until very recently, is a fact I leave to be explained on further investigation. The word is an old one and a good one, but I fancy that its use in England could not have been generally diffused in the seventeenth century. So a Hoosier or a Kentuckian never *pared* an apple, but *peeled* it. Much light might be thrown on the origin and history of our dialects by investigating their deficiencies.

could have been had he been a criminal. And this sudden and morbid sense of his guilt as it appeared to Hannah paralyzed him. But when Hannah lifted her bucket with her hand, and the world with her heavy heart, and essayed to pass him, Ralph rallied and said:

"*You* don't believe all these lies that are told about me."

"I don't believe anything, Mr. Hartsook; that is, I don't want to believe anything against you. And I wouldn't mind anything they say if it wasn't for two things"—here she stammered and looked down.

"If it wasn't for what?" said Ralph with a spice of indignant denial in his voice.

Hannah hesitated, but Ralph pressed the question with eagerness.

"I saw you cross that blue-grass pasture the night—the night that you walked home with me." She would have said the night of the robbery, but her heart smote her, and she adopted the more kindly form of the sentence.

Ralph would have explained, but how?

"I did cross the pasture," he began, "but——"

Just here it occurred to Ralph that there was no reason for his night excursion across the pasture. Hannah again took up her bucket, but he said:

"Tell me what else you have against me."

"I haven't anything against you. Only I am poor and friendless, and you oughtn't to make my life any heavier. They say that you have paid attention to a great many girls. I don't know why you should want to trifle with me."

Ralph answered her this time. He spoke low. He spoke as though he were speaking to God. "If any man says that I ever trifled with any woman, he lies. I have never loved but one, and you know who that is. And God knows."

"I don't know what to say, Mr. Hartsook." Hannah's voice was broken. These solemn words of love were like a river in the desert, and she was like a wanderer dying of thirst. "I don't know, Mr. Hartsook. If I was alone, it wouldn't matter. But I've got my blind mother and my poor Shocky to look after. And I don't want to make mistakes. And the world is so full of lies I don't know what to believe. Somehow I can't help believing what you say. You seem to speak so true. But——"

"But what?" said Ralph.

"But you know how I saw you just as kind to Martha Hawkins on Sunday as—as——"

"Han—ner!" It was the melodious voice of the angry Mrs. Means, and Hannah lifted her pail and disappeared.

Standing in the shadow of his own despair, Ralph felt how dark a night could be when it had no promise of morning.

And Dr. Small, who had been stabling his horse just inside the barn, came out and moved quietly into the house just as though he had not listened intently to every word of the conversation.

As Ralph walked away he tried to comfort himself by calling to his aid the bulldog in his character. But somehow it did not do him any good. For what is a bulldog but a stoic philosopher? Stoicism has its value, but Ralph had come to a place where stoicism was of no account. The memory of the Helper, of his sorrow, his brave and victorious endurance, came when stoicism failed. Happiness might go out of life, but in the light of Christ's life happiness seemed but a small element anyhow. The love of woman might be denied him, but there still remained what was infinitely more precious and holy, the love of God. There still remained the possibility of heroic living. Working, suffering, and enduring still remained. And he who can work for God and endure for God, surely has yet the best of life left. And, like the knights who could find the Holy Grail only in losing themselves, Hartsook, in throwing his happiness out of the count, found the purest happiness, a sense of the victory of the soul over the tribulations of life. The man who knows this victory scarcely needs the encouragement of the hope of future happiness. There is a real heaven in bravely lifting the load of one's own sorrow and work.

And it was a good thing for Ralph that the danger hanging over Shocky made immediate action necessary.

CHAPTER XX

GOD REMEMBERS SHOCKY

At four o'clock the next morning, in the midst of a driving snow, Ralph went timidly up the lane toward the homely castle of the Meanses. He went timidly, for he was afraid of Bull. But he found Bud waiting for him, with the roan colt bridled and saddled. The roan colt was really a large three-year-old, full of the finest sort of animal life, and having, as Bud declared, "a mighty sight of hoss sense fer his age." He seemed to understand at once that there was something extraordinary on hand when he was brought out of his comfortable quarters at four in the morning in the midst of a snow-storm. Bud was sure that the roan colt felt his responsibility.

In the days that followed, Ralph often had occasion to remember this interview with Bud, who had risked much in bringing his fractured arm out into the cold, damp air. Jonathan never clave to David more earnestly than did Bud this December morning to Ralph.

"You see, Mr. Hartsook," said Bud, "I wish I was well myself. It's hard to set still. But it's a-doing me a heap of good. I'm like a boy at school. And I'm a-findin' out that doing one's best licks fer others ain't all they is of it, though it's a good part.

I feel like as if I must git Him, you know, to do lots for me. They's always some sums too hard fer a feller, and he has to ax the master to do 'em, you know. But see, the roan's a-stomping round. He wants to be off. Do you know I think that hoss knows something's up? I think he puts in his best licks fer me a good deal better than I do fer Him."

Ralph pressed Bud's right hand. Bud rubbed his face against the colt's nose and said: "Put in your best licks, old fellow." And the colt whinnied. How a horse must want to speak! For Bud was right. Men are gods to horses, and they serve their deities with a faithfulness that shames us.

Then Ralph sprang into the saddle, and the roan, as if wishing to show Bud his willingness, broke into a swinging gallop, and was soon lost to the sight of his master in the darkness and the snow. When Bud could no more hear the sound of the roan's footsteps he returned to the house, to lie awake picturing to himself the journey of Ralph with Shocky and the roan colt. It was a great comfort to Bud that the roan, which was almost a part of himself, represented him in this ride. And he knew the roan well enough to feel sure that he would do credit to his master. "He'll put in his best licks," Bud whispered to himself many a time before daybreak.

The ground was but little frozen, and the snow made the roads more slippery than ever. But the rough-shod roan handled his feet dexterously and with a playful and somewhat self-righteous air, as though he said: "Didn't I do it handsomely that time?" Down slippery hills, through deep mud-holes covered with a slender film of ice he trod with perfect assurance. And then up over the rough stones of Rocky Hollow, where there was no road at all, he picked his way through the darkness and snow. Ralph could not tell where he was at last, but gave the reins to the roan, who did his duty bravely, and not without a little flourish, to show that he had yet plenty of spare power.

A feeble candle-ray, making the dense snow-fall visible, marked for Ralph the site of the basket-maker's cabin. Miss Martha had been admitted to the secret, and had joined in the conspiracy heartily, without being able to recall anything of the kind having occurred at the East, and not re-membering having seen or heard of anything of the sort the time she was to Bosting. She had Shocky all ready, having used some of her own capes and shawls to make him warm.

Miss Martha came out to meet Ralph when she heard the feet of the roan before the door.

"O Mr. Hartsook! is that you? What a storm! This is jest the way it snows at the East. Shocky's all ready. He didn't know a thing about it tell I waked him this morning. Ever since that he's been saying that God hasn't forgot, after all. It's made me cry more'n once." And Shocky kissed Mrs. Pearson, and told her that when he got away from Flat Creek he'd tell God all about it, and God would bring Mr. Pearson back again. And then Martha Hawkins lifted the frail little form, bundled in shawls, in her arms, and brought him out into the storm; and before she handed him up he embraced her, and said: "O Miss Hawkins! God ha'n't forgot me, after all. Tell Hanner that He ha'n't forgot. I'm going to ask Him to git her away from Means's and mother out of the poor-house. I'll ask Him just as soon as I get to Lewisburg."

Ralph lifted the trembling form into his arms, and the little fellow only looked up in the face of the master and said: "You see, Mr. Hartsook, I thought God had forgot. But He ha'n't."

And the words of the little boy comforted the master also. God had not forgotten him, either!

From the moment that Ralph took Shocky into his arms, the conduct of the roan colt underwent an entire revolution. Before that he had gone over a bad place with a rush, as though he were ambitious of distinguishing himself by his brilliant execution. Now he trod none the less surely, but he trod tenderly. The neck was no longer arched. He set himself to his work as steadily as though he were twenty years old. For miles he traveled on in a long, swinging walk, putting his feet down carefully and firmly. And Ralph found the spirit of the colt entering into himself. He cut the snow-storm with his face, and felt a sense of triumph over all his difficulties. The bulldog's jaws had been his teacher, and now the steady, strong, and conscientious legs of the roan inspired him.

Shocky had not spoken. He lay listening to the pattering music of the horse's feet, doubtless framing the footsteps of the roan colt into an anthem of praise to the God who had not forgot. But as the

dawn came on, making the snow whiter, he raised
himself and said half-aloud, as he watched the flakes
chasing one another in whirling eddies, that the
snow seemed to be having a good time of it. Then
he leaned down again on the master's bosom, full of
a still joy, and only roused himself from his happy
reverie to ask what that big, ugly-looking house was.

"See, Mr. Hartsook, how big it is, and how little
and ugly the windows is! And the boards is peel-
ing off all over it, and the hogs is right in the front
yard. It don't look just like a house. It looks
dreadful. What is it?"

Ralph had dreaded this question. He did not
answer it, but asked Shocky to change his position
a little, and then he quickened the pace of the horse.
But Shocky was a poet, and a poet understands
silence more quickly than he does speech. The
little fellow shivered as the truth came to him.

"Is that the poor-house?" he said, catching his
breath. "Is my mother in that place? *Won't* you
take me in there, so as I can just kiss her once?
'Cause she can't see much, you know. And one
kiss from me will make her feel so good. And I'll
tell her that God ha'n't forgot." He had raised
up and caught hold of Ralph's coat.

Ralph had great difficulty in quieting him. He
told him that if he went in there Bill Jones might
claim that he was a runaway and belonged there.
And poor Shocky only shivered and said he was
cold. A minute later, Ralph found that he was
shaking with a chill, and a horrible dread came
over him. What if Shocky should die? It was

only a minute's work to get down, take the warm horse-blanket from under the saddle, and wrap it about the boy, then to strip off his own overcoat and add that to it. It was now daylight, and finding, after he had mounted, that Shocky continued to shiver, he put the roan to his best speed for the rest of the way, trotting up and down the slippery hills, and galloping away on the level ground. How bravely the roan laid himself to his work, making the fence-corners fly past in a long procession! But poor little Shocky was too cold to notice them, and Ralph shuddered lest Shocky should never be warm again, and spoke to the roan, and the roan stretched out his head, and dropped one ear back to hear the first word of command, and stretched the other forward to listen for danger, and then flew with a splendid speed down the road, past the patches of blackberry briars, past the elderberry bushes, past the familiar red-haw tree in the fence-corner, over the bridge without regard to the threat of a five-dollar fine, and at last up the long lane into the village, where the smoke from the chimneys was caught and whirled round with the snow.

CHAPTER XXI

MISS NANCY SAWYER

In a little old cottage in Lewisburg, on one of the streets which was never traveled except by a solitary cow seeking pasture or a countryman bringing wood to some one of the half-dozen families living in it, and which in summer was decked with a profusion of the yellow and white blossoms of the dog-fennel—in this unfrequented street, so generously and unnecessarily broad, lived Miss Nancy Sawyer and her younger sister Semantha. Miss Nancy was a providence, one of those old maids that are benedictions to the whole town; one of those in whom the mother-love, wanting the natural objects on which to spend itself, overflows all bounds and lavishes itself on every needy thing, and grows richer and more abundant with the spending, a fountain of inexhaustible blessing. There is no nobler life possible to any one than to an unmarried woman. The more shame that some choose a selfish one, and thus turn to gall all the affection with which they are endowed. Miss Nancy Sawyer had been Ralph's Sunday-school teacher, and it was precious little, so far as information went, that he learned from her; for she never could conceive of Jerusalem as a place in any essential regard very different from Lewisburg, where she had spent her life. But Ralph learned from her what most Sunday-school teachers fail to teach, the great lesson of Christianity, by the side of which all antiquities and geographies and chronologies and exegetics and other niceties are as nothing.

And now he turned the head of the roan toward the cottage of Miss Nancy Sawyer as naturally as the roan would have gone to his own stall in the stable at home. The snow had gradually ceased to fall, and was eddying round the house, when Ralph dismounted from his foaming horse, and, carrying the still form of Shocky as reverently as though it had been something heavenly, knocked at Miss Nancy Sawyer's door.

With natural feminine instinct that lady started back when she saw Hartsook, for she had just built a fire in the stove, and she now stood at the door with unwashed face and uncombed hair.

"Why, Ralph Hartsook, where did you drop down from—and what have you got?"

"I came from Flat Creek this morning, and I brought you a little angel who has got out of heaven, and needs some of your motherly care."

Shocky was brought in. The chill shook him now by fits only, for a fever had spotted his cheeks already.

"Who are you?" said Miss Nancy, as she unwrapped him.

"I'm Shocky, a little boy as God forgot, and then thought of again."

CHAPTER XXII

PANCAKES

HALF an hour later, Ralph, having seen Miss Nancy Sawyer's machinery of warm baths and simple remedies safely in operation, and having seen the roan colt comfortably stabled, and rewarded for his faithfulness by a bountiful supply of the best hay and the promise of oats when he was cool—half an hour later Ralph was doing the most ample, satisfactory, and amazing justice to his Aunt Matilda's hot buckwheat-cakes and warm coffee. And after his life in Flat Creek, Aunt Matilda's house did look like paradise. How white the table-cloth, how bright the coffee-pot, how clean the wood-work, how glistening the brass door-knobs, how spotless everything that came under the sovereign sway of Mrs. Matilda White! For in every Indiana village as large as Lewisburg, there are generally a half-dozen women who are admitted to be the best housekeepers. All others are only imitators. And the strife is between these for the pre-eminence. It is at least safe to say that no other in Lewisburg stood so high as an enemy to dirt, and as a "rat, roach, and mouse exterminator," as did Mrs. Matilda White, the wife of Ralph's maternal uncle, Robert White, Esq., a lawyer in successful practice. Of course no member of Mrs. White's family ever stayed at home longer than was necessary. Her husband found his office—which he kept in as bad a state as possible in order to maintain an equilibrium in his life—much more comfortable than the stiffly clean house at home. From the time that Ralph had come to live as a chore-boy at his uncle's, he had ever crossed the threshold of Aunt Matilda's temple of cleanliness with a horrible sense of awe. And Walter Johnson, her son by a former marriage, had—poor, weak-willed fellow!—been driven into bad company and bad habits by the wretchedness of extreme civilization. And yet he showed the hereditary trait, for all the genius which Mrs. White consecrated to the glorious work of making her house too neat to be habitable, her son Walter gave to tying exquisite knots in his colored cravats and combing his oiled locks so as to look like a dandy barber. And she had no other children. The kind Providence that watches over the destiny of children takes care that very few of them are lodged in these terribly clean houses.

But Walter was not at the table, and Ralph had so much anxiety lest his absence should be significant of evil, that he did not venture to inquire after him as he sat there between Mr. and Mrs. White disposing of Aunt Matilda's cakes with an appetite only justified by his long morning's ride and the excellence of the brown cakes, the golden honey, and the coffee, enriched, as Aunt Matilda's always was, with the most generous cream. Aunt Matilda was so absorbed in telling of the doings of the Dorcas Society that she entirely forgot to be surprised at the early hour of Ralph's arrival. When she had described the number of the garments finished to be sent to the Five Points Mission, or the Home for the Friendless, or the South Sea Islands, I forget which, Ralph thought he saw his chance, while Aunt Matilda was in a benevolent mood, to broach a plan he had been revolving for some time. But when he looked at Aunt Matilda's immaculate— horribly immaculate—housekeeping, his heart failed him, and he would have said nothing had she not inadvertently opened the door herself.

"How did you get here so early, Ralph?" and Aunt Matilda's face was shadowed with a coming rebuke.

"By early rising," said Ralph. But, seeing the gathering frown on his aunt's brow, he hastened to tell the story of Shocky as well as he could. Mrs. White did not give way to any impulse toward sympathy until she learned that Shocky was safely housed with Miss Nancy Sawyer.

"Yes, Sister Sawyer has no family cares," she said by way of smoothing her slightly ruffled complacency, "she has no family cares, and she can do those things. Sometimes I think she lets people impose on her and keep her away from the means of grace, and I spoke to our new preacher about it the last time he was here, and asked him to speak to Sister Sawyer about staying away from the ordinances to wait on everybody, but he is a queer man, and he only said that he supposed Sister Sawyer neglected the inferior ordinances that she might attend to higher ones. But I don't see any sense in a minister of the gospel calling prayer-meeting a lower ordinance than feeding catnip-tea to Mrs. Brown's last baby. But hasn't this little boy—Shocking, or what do you call him?—got any mother?"

"Yes," said Ralph, "and that was just what I was going to say." And he proceeded to tell how anxious Shocky was to see his half-blind mother, and actually ventured to wind up his remarks by suggesting that Shocky's mother be invited to stay over Sunday in Aunt Matilda's house.

"Bless my stars!" said that astounded saint, "fetch a pauper here? What crazy notions you have got! Fetch her here out of the poor-house? Why, she wouldn't be fit to sleep in my——" here Aunt Matilda choked. The bare thought of having a pauper in her billowy beds, whose snowy whiteness was frightful to any ordinary mortal, the bare thought of the contagion of the poor-house taking possession of one of her beds, smothered her. "And then you know sore eyes are very catching."

Ralph boiled a little. "Aunt Matilda, do you think Dorcas was afraid of sore eyes?"

It was a center shot, and the lawyer-uncle, lawyerlike, enjoyed a good hit. And he enjoyed a good hit at his wife best of all, for he never ventured on one himself. But Aunt Matilda felt that a direct reply was impossible. She was not a lawyer but a woman, and so dodged the question by making a counter-charge.

"It seems to me, Ralph, that you have picked up some very low associates. And you go around at

night, I am told. You get over here by daylight,
and I hear that you have made common cause with
a lame soldier who acts as a spy for thieves, and
that your running about of night is likely to get
you into trouble."

Ralph was hit this time. "I suppose," he said,
"that you've been listening to some of Henry Small's
lies."

"Why, Ralph, how you talk! The worst sign of
all is that you abuse such a young man as Dr. Small,
the most exemplary Christian young man in the
county. And he is a great friend of yours, for when
he was here last week he did not say a word against
you, but looked so sorry when your being in trouble
was mentioned. Didn't he, Mr. White?"

Mr. White, as in duty bound, said yes, but he
said yes in a cool, lawyerlike way, which showed
that he did not take quite so much stock in Dr.
Small as his wife did. This was a comfort to Ralph,
who sat picturing to himself the silent flattery
which Dr. Small's eyes paid to his Aunt Matilda,
and the quiet expression of pain that would flit
across his face when Ralph's name was mentioned.
And never until that moment had Hartsook understood how masterful Small's artifices were. He had
managed to elevate himself in Mrs. White's estima-
tion and to destroy Ralph at the same time, and had
managed to do both by a contraction of the
eyebrows!

But the silence was growing painful and Ralph
thought to break it and turn the current of talk
from himself by asking after Mrs. White's son.

"Where is Walter?"

"Oh! Walter's doing well. He went down to Clifty three weeks ago to study medicine with Henry Small. He seems so fond of the doctor, and the doctor is such an excellent man, you know, and I have strong hopes that Wallie will be led to see the error of his ways by his association with Henry. I suppose he would have gone to see you but for the unfavorable reports that he heard. I hope, Ralph, you too will make the friendship of Dr. Small. And for the sake of your poor, dead mother"—here Aunt Matilda endeavored to show some emotion— "for the sake of your poor, dead mother——"

But Ralph heard no more. The buckwheat-cakes had lost their flavor. He remembered that the colt had not yet had his oats, and so, in the very midst of Aunt Matilda's affecting allusion to his mother, like a stiff-necked reprobate that he was, Ralph Hartsook rose abruptly from the table, put on his hat, and went out toward the stable.

"I declare," said Mrs. White, descending suddenly from her high moral stand-point, "I declare that boy has stepped right on the threshold of the back-door," and she stuffed her white handkerchief into her pocket, and took down the floor-cloth to wipe off the imperceptible blemish left by Ralph's boot-heels. And Mr. White followed his nephew to the stable to request that he would be a little careful what he did about anybody in the poor-house, as any trouble with the Joneses might defeat Mr. White's nomination to the judgeship of the Court of Common Pleas.

CHAPTER XXIII

A CHARITABLE INSTITUTION

WHEN Ralph got back to Miss Nancy Sawyer's, Shocky was sitting up in bed talking to Miss Nancy and Miss Semantha. His cheeks were a little flushed with fever and the excitement of telling his story; theirs were wet with tears. "Ralph," whispered Miss Nancy, as she drew him into the kitchen, "I want you to get a buggy or a sleigh, and go right over to the poor-house and fetch that boy's mother over here. It'll do me more good than any sermon I ever heard to see that boy in his mother's arms to-morrow. We can keep the old lady over Sunday."

Ralph was delighted, so delighted that he came near kissing good Miss Nancy Sawyer, whose plain face was glorified by her generosity.

But he did not go to the poor-house immediately. He waited until he saw Bill Jones, the Superintendent of the Poor-House, and Pete Jones, the County Commissioner, who was still somewhat shuck up, ride up to the court-house. Then he drove out of the village, and presently hitched his horse to the poor-house fence, and took a survey of the outside. Forty hogs, nearly ready for slaughter, wallowed in a pen in front of the forlorn and dilapidated house; for though the commissioners allowed a claim for repairs at every meeting, the repairs were never made, and it would not do to scrutinize Mr. Jones's bills too closely, unless you gave up all hope of renomination to office. One curious effect of political aspirations in Hoopole County, was to shut the eyes that they could not see, to close the ears that they could not hear, and to destroy the sense of smell. But Ralph, not being a politician smelled the hog-pen without and the stench within, and saw everywhere the transparent fraud, and heard the echo of Jones's cruelty.

A weak-eyed girl admitted him, and as he did not wish to make his business known at once, he affected a sort of idle interest in the place, and asked to be allowed to look round. The weak-eyed girl watched him. He found that all the women with children, twenty persons in all, were obliged to sleep in one room, which, owing to the hill-slope, was partly under ground, and which had but half a window for light, and no ventilation, except the chance draft from the door. Jones had declared that the women with children must stay there—"he warn't goin' to have brats a-runnin' over the whole house." Here were vicious women and good women, with their children, crowded like chickens in a coop for market. And there were, as usual in such places, helpless, idiotic women with illegitimate children. Of course this room was the scene of perpetual quarreling and occasional fighting.

In the quarters devoted to the insane, people slightly demented and raving maniacs were in the same rooms, while there were also those utter wrecks which sat in heaps on the floor, mumbling and

muttering unintelligible words, the whole current
of their thoughts hopelessly muddled, turning around
upon itself in eddies never ending.

"That air woman," said the weak-eyed girl, "used
to holler a heap when she was brought in here. But
Pap knows how to subjue 'em. He slapped her in
the mouth every time she hollered. She don't make
no furss now, but jist sets down that way all day,
and keeps a-whisperin'."

Ralph understood it. When she came in she was
the victim of mania; but she had been beaten into
hopeless idiocy. Indeed this state of incurable im-
becility seemed the end toward which all traveled.
Shut in these bare rooms, with no treatment, no
exercise, no variety, and meager food, cases of
slight derangement soon grew into chronic lunacy.

One young woman, called Phil, a sweet-faced
person, apparently a farmer's wife, came up to
Ralph and looked at him kindly, playing with the
buttons on his coat in a childlike simplicity. Her
blue-drilling dress was sewed all over with patches
of white, representing ornamental buttons. The
womanly instinct toward adornment had in her
taken this childish turn.

"Don't you think they ought to let me go home?"
she said with a sweetness and a wistful, longing,
home-sick look, that touched Ralph to the heart.
He looked at her, and then at the muttering crones,
and he could see no hope of any better fate for her.
She followed him round the barn-like rooms, re-
turning every now and then to her question, "Don't
you think I might go home now?"

The weak-eyed girl had been called away for a moment, and Ralph stood looking into a cell, where there was a man with a gay red plume in his hat and a strip of red flannel about his waist. He strutted up and down like a drill-sergeant.

"I am General Andrew Jackson," he began. "People don't believe it, but I am. I had my head shot off at Bueny Visty, and the new one that growed on isn't nigh so good as the old one; it's tater on one side.[1] That's why they take advantage of me to shut me up. But I know some things. My head is tater on one side, but it's all right on t'other. And when I know a thing in the left side of my head, I know it. Lean down here. Let me tell you something out of the left side. Not out of the tater side, mind ye. I wouldn't a told you if he hadn't locked me up fer nothing. *Bill Jones is a thief!* He sells the bodies of the dead paupers, and then sells the empty coffins back to the county agin. But that a'n't all—"

Just then the weak-eyed girl came back, and, as Ralph moved away, General Jackson called out: "That a'n't all. I'll tell the rest another time. And that a'n't out of the tater side, you can depend on that. That's out of the left side. Sound as a nut on that side!"

---

[1] Some time after this book appeared Dr. Brown-Séquard announced his theory of the dual brain. A writer in an English magazine called attention to the fact that the discovery had been anticipated by an imaginative writer, and cited the passage in the text as proving that the author of "The Hoosier School-master" had outrun Dr. Brown-Séquard in perceiving the duality of the brain. It is a matter for surprise that an author, even an "imaginative" one, should have made so great a discovery without suspecting its meaning until it was explained by some one else.

But Ralph began to wonder where he should find Hannah's mother.

"Don't go in there," cried the weak-eyed girl, as Ralph was opening a door. "Ole Mowley's in there, and she'll cuss you."

"Oh! well, if that's all, her curses won't hurt," said Hartsook, pushing open the door. But the volley of blasphemy and vile language that he received made him stagger. The old hag paced the floor, abusing everybody that came in her way. And by the window, in the same room, feeling the light that struggled through the dusty glass upon her face, sat a sorrowful, intelligent Englishwoman. Ralph noticed at once that she was English, and in a few moments he discovered that her sight was defective. Could it be that Hannah's mother was the room-mate of this loathsome creature, whose profanity and obscenity did not intermit for a moment?

Happily the weak-eyed girl had not dared to brave the curses of Mowley. Ralph stepped forward to the woman by the window, and greeted her.

"Is this Mrs. Thomson?"

"That is my name, sir," she said, turning her face toward Ralph, who could not but remark the contrast between the thorough refinement of her manner and her coarse, scant, unshaped pauper-frock of blue drilling.

"I saw your daughter yesterday."

"Did you see my boy?"

There was a tremulousness in her voice and an agitation in her manner which disclosed the emotion she strove in vain to conceal. For only the day before Bill Jones had informed her that Shocky would be bound out on Saturday, and that she would find that goin' agin him warn't a payin' business, so much as some others he mout mention.

Ralph told her about Shocky's safety. I shall not write down the conversation here. Critics would say that it was an overwrought scene. As if all the world were as cold as they! All I can tell is that this refined woman had all she could do to control herself in her eagerness to get out of her prison-house, away from the blasphemies of Mowley, away from the insults of Jones, away from the sights and sounds and smells of the place, and, above all, her eagerness to fly to the little shocky-head from whom she had been banished for two years. It seemed to her that she could gladly die now, if she could die with that flaxen head upon her bosom.

And so, in spite of the opposition of Bill Jones's son, who threatened her with every sort of evil if she left, Ralph wrapped Mrs. Thomson's blue drilling in Nancy Sawyer's shawl, and bore the feeble woman off to Lewisburg. And as they drove away, a sad, childlike voice cried from the gratings of the upper window, "Good-by! good-by!" Ralph turned and saw that it was Phil, poor Phil, for whom there was no deliverance.[1] And all the way back Ralph pronounced mental maledictions on the Dorcas Society, not for sending garments to the Five Points

---

[1] The reader may be interested to know that "Phil" was drawn from the life, as was old Mowley and in part "General Jackson" also. Between 1867 and 1870, I visited many jails and poor-houses with philanthropic purpose, publishing the results of my examination in some cases in *The Chicago Tribune*. Some of the abuses pointed out were reformed, others linger till this day, I believe.

or the South Sea Islands, whichever it was, but for being so blind to the sorrow and poverty within its reach. He did not know, for he had not read the reports of the Boards of State Charities, that nearly all alms-houses are very much like this, and that the State of New York is not better in this regard than Indiana. And he did not know that it is true in almost all other counties, as it was in his own, that "Christian" people do not think enough of Christ to look for him in these lazar-houses.

And while Ralph denounced the Dorcas Society, the eager, hungry heart of the mother ran, flew toward the little white-headed boy.

No, I can not do it; I can not tell you about that meeting. I am sure that Miss Nancy Sawyer's tea tasted exceedingly good to the pauper, who had known nothing but cold water for years, and that the bread and butter were delicious to a palate that had eaten poor-house soup for dinner, and coarse poor-house bread and vile molasses for supper, and that without change for three years. But I can not tell you how it seemed that evening to Miss Nancy Sawyer, as the poor English lady sat in speechless ecstacy, rocking in the old splint-bottomed rocking-chair in the fire-light, while she pressed to her bosom with all the might of her enfeebled arms, the form of the little Shocky, who half-sobbed and half-sang, over and over again, "God ha'n't forgot us, mother; God ha'n't forgot us."

CHAPTER XXIV

THE GOOD SAMARITAN

The Methodist church to which Mrs. Matilda White and Miss Nancy Sawyer belonged was the leading one in Lewisburg, as it was in most county-seat villages in Indiana. If I may be permitted to express my candid and charitable opinion of the difference between the two women, I shall have to use the old Quaker locution, and say that Miss Sawyer was a Methodist and likewise a Christian; Mrs. White was a Methodist, but I fear she was not likewise.

As to the first part of this assertion, there was no room to doubt Miss Nancy's piety. She could get happy in class-meeting (for who had a better right?), and could witness a good experience in the quarterly love-feast. But it is not upon these grounds that I base my opinion of Miss Nancy. Do not even the Pharisees the same? She never dreamed that she had any right to speak of "Christian Perfection" (which, as Mrs. Partington said of total depravity, is an excellent doctrine if it is lived up to); but when a woman's heart is full of devout affections and good purposes, when her head devises liberal and Christ-like things, when her hands are always open to the poor and always busy with acts of love and self-denial, and when her feet are ever eager to run upon errands of mercy, why, if there be anything worthy of being called Christian Perfection in this world of imperfection, I do not know why such an one does not possess it. What need of analyzing her experiences *in vacuo* to find out the state of her soul?

How Miss Nancy managed to live on her slender income and be so generous was a perpetual source of perplexity to the gossips of Lewisburg. And now that she declared that Mrs. Thomson and Shocky should not return to the poor-house there was a general outcry from the whole Committee of Intermeddlers that she would bring herself to the poor-house before she died. But Nancy Sawyer was the richest woman in Lewisburg, though nobody knew it, and though she herself did not once suspect it.

How Miss Nancy and the preacher conspired together, and how they managed to bring Mrs. Thomson's case up at the time of the "Sacramental Service" in the afternoon of that Sunday in Lewisburg, and how the preacher made a touching statement of it just before the regular "Collection for the Poor" was taken, and how the warm-hearted Methodists put in dollars instead of dimes while the Presiding Elder read those passages about Zaccheus and other liberal people, and how the congregation sang

"He dies, the Friend of sinners dies"

more lustily than ever, after having performed this Christian act—how all this happened I can not take up the reader's time to tell. But I can assure him that the nearly blind English woman did not room

with blasphemous old Mowley any more, and that
the blue-drilling pauper frock gave way to something better, and that grave little Shocky even
danced with delight, and declared that God hadn't
forgot, though he'd thought that He had. And
Mrs. Matilda White remarked that it was a shame
that the collection for the poor at a Methodist sacramental service should be given to a woman who
was a member of the Church of England, and like
as not never soundly converted!

And Shocky slept in his mother's arms and prayed
God not to forget Hannah, while Shocky's mother
knit stockings for the store day and night, and day
and night she prayed and hoped.

CHAPTER XXV

BUD WOOING

THE Sunday that Ralph spent in Lewisburg, the Sunday that Shocky spent in an earthly paradise, the Sunday that Mrs. Thomson spent with Shocky instead of old Mowley, the Sunday that Miss Nancy thought was "just like heaven," was also an eventful Sunday with Bud Means. He had long adored Miss Martha in his secret heart, but, like many other giants, while brave enough to face and fight dragons, he was a coward in the presence of the woman that he loved. Let us honor him for it. The man who loves a woman truly, reverences her profoundly and feels abashed in her presence. The man who is never abashed in the presence of womanhood, the man who tells his love without a tremor, is a shallow egotist. Bud's nature was not fine. But it was deep, true, and manly. To him Martha Hawkins was the chief of women. What was he that he should aspire to possess her? And yet on that Sunday, with his crippled arm carefully bound up, with his cleanest shirt, and with his heavy boots freshly oiled with the fat of the raccoon, he started hopefully through fields white with snow to the house of Squire Hawkins. When he started his spirits were high, but they descended exactly in proportion to his proximity to the object of his love. He thought himself not dressed well enough. He wished his shoulders were not so square, and his arms not so stout. He wished that he had book-larnin' enough to court in nice, big words. And so, by recounting his own deficiencies, he succeeded in making himself feel weak, and awkward, and generally good-for-nothing, by the time he walked up between the rows of dead hollyhocks to the Squire's front door, to tap at which took all his remaining strength.

Miss Martha received her perspiring lover most graciously, but this only convinced Bud more than ever that she was a superior being. If she had slighted him a bit, so as to awaken his combativeness, his bashfulness might have disappeared.

It was in vain that Martha inquired about his arm and complimented his courage. Bud could only think of his big feet, his clumsy hands, and his slow tongue. He answered in monosyllables, using his red silk handkerchief diligently.

"Is your arm improving?" asked Miss Hawkins.

"Yes, I think it is," said Bud, hastily crossing his right leg over his left, and trying to get his fists out of sight.

"Have you heard from Mr. Pearson?"

"No, I ha'n't," answered Bud, removing his right foot to the floor again, because it looked so big, and trying to push his left hand into his pocket.

"Beautiful sunshine, isn't it?" said Martha.

"Yes, 'tis," answered Bud, sticking his right foot up on the rung of the chair and putting his right hand behind him.

"This snow looks like the snow we have at the

East," said Martha. "It snowed that way the time I was to Bosting."

"Did it?" said Bud, not thinking of the snow at all nor of Boston, but thinking how much better he would have appeared had he left his arms and legs at home.

"I suppose Mr. Hartsook rode your horse to Lewisburg?"

"Yes, he did;" and Bud hung both hands at his side.

"You were very kind."

This set Bud's heart a-going so that he could not say anything, but he looked eloquently at Miss Hawkins, drew both feet under the chair, and rammed his hands into his pockets. Then, suddenly remembering how awkward he must look, he immediately pulled his hands out again, and crossed his legs. There was a silence of a few minutes, during which Bud made up his mind to do the most desperate thing he could think of—to declare his love and take the consequences.

"You see, Miss Hawkins," he began, forgetting boots and fists in his agony, "I thought as how I'd come over here to-day, and"—but here his heart failed him utterly—"and—see—you."

"I'm glad to see you, Mr. Means."

"And I thought I'd tell you"—Martha was sure it was coming now, for Bud was in dead earnest— "and I thought I'd just like to tell you, ef I only know'd jest how to tell it right"—here Bud got frightened, and did not dare close the sentence as he had intended—"I thought as how you might like

to know—or ruther I wanted to tell you—that—the
—that I—that we—all of us—think—that—I—that
we are going to have a spellin'-school a Chewsday
night."

"I'm real glad to hear it," said the bland but disappointed Martha. "We used to have spelling-
schools at the East." But Miss Martha could not
remember that they had them "to Bosting."

Hard as it is for a bashful man to talk, it is still
more difficult for him to close the conversation.
Most men like to leave a favorable impression, and
a bashful man is always waiting with the forlorn
hope that some favorable turn in the talk may let
him out without absolute discomfiture. And so
Bud stayed a long time, and how he ever did get
away he never could tell.

CHAPTER XXVI

A LETTER AND ITS CONSEQUENCES

"Squar Haukins

"this is too Lett u no that u beter be Keerful hoo yoo an yore familly tacks cides with fer peepl wont Stan it too hev the Men wat's sportin the wuns wat's robin us, sported bi yor Fokes kepin kumpne with 'em, u been a ossifer ov the Lau, yor Ha wil bern as qick as to an yor Barn tu. so Tak kere. No mor ad pressnt."

This letter accomplished its purpose. The Squire's spectacles slipped off several times while he read it. His wig had to be adjusted. If he had been threatened personally he would not have minded it so much. But the hay-stacks were dearer to him than the apple of his glass eye. The barn was more precious than his wig. And those who hoped to touch Bud in a tender place through this letter knew the Squire's weakness far better than they knew the spelling-book. To see his new red barn with its large "Mormon" hay-press inside, and the mounted Indian on the vane, consumed, was too much for the Hawkins heart to stand. Evidently the danger was on the side of his niece. But how should he influence Martha to give up Bud? Martha did not value the hay-stacks half so highly as she did her lover. Martha did not think the new red barn, with the great Mormon press inside and the galloping Indian on the vane, worth half so much as a moral principle or a kind-hearted action. Martha, bless her! would have sacrificed anything rather than forsake the poor. But Squire Hawkins's lips shut tight over his false teeth in a way that suggested astringent purse-strings, and Squire Hawkins could not sleep at night if the new red barn, with the galloping Indian on the vane, were in danger. Martha must be reached somehow.

So, with many adjustings of that most adjustable wig, with many turnings of that reversible glass eye, the Squire managed to frighten Martha by the intimation that he had been threatened, and to make her understand, what it cost her much to understand, that she must turn the cold shoulder to chivalrous, awkward Bud, whom she loved most tenderly, partly, perhaps, because he did not remind her of anybody she had ever known at the East.

Tuesday evening was the fatal time. Spelling-school was the fatal occasion. Bud was the victim. Pete Jones had his revenge. For Bud had been all the evening trying to muster courage enough to offer himself as Martha's escort. He was not encouraged by the fact that he had spelled even worse than usual, while Martha had distinguished herself by holding her ground against Jeems Phillips for half an hour. But he screwed his courage to the sticking place, not by quoting to himself the adage, "Faint heart never won fair lady," which, indeed, he had never heard, but by reminding himself that "ef you don't resk nothin' you'll never git nothin'." So, when the spelling-school had adjourned, he sidled up to her, and, looking dreadfully solemn and a little foolish, he said:

"Kin I see you safe home?"

And she, with a feeling that her uncle's life was in danger, and that his salvation depended upon her resolution—she, with a feeling that she was pronouncing sentence of death on her own great hope, answered huskily:

"No, I thank you."

If she had only known that it was the red barn with the Indian on top that was in danger, she would probably have let the galloping brave take care of himself.

It seemed to Bud, as he walked home mortified, disgraced, disappointed, hopeless, that all the world had gone down in a whirlpool of despair.

"Might a knowed it," he said to himself. "Of course, a smart gal like Martha a'n't agoin' to take a big, blunderin' fool that can't spell in two sylla-bles. What's the use of tryin'? A Flat Cricker is a Flat Cricker. You can't make nothin' else out of him, no more nor you can make a Chiny hog into a Berkshire."

CHAPTER XXVII

A LOSS AND A GAIN

DR. SMALL, silent, attentive, assiduous Dr. Small set himself to work to bind up the wounded heart of Bud Means, even as he had bound up his broken arm. The flattery of his fine eyes, which looked at Bud's muscles so admiringly, which gave attention to his lightest remark, was not lost on the young Flat Creek Hercules. Outwardly at least Pete Jones showed no inclination to revenge himself on Bud. Was it respect for muscle, or was it the influence of Small? At any rate, the concentrated extract of the resentment of Pete Jones and his clique was now ready to empty itself upon the head of Hartsook. And Ralph found himself in his dire extremity without even the support of Bud, whose good resolutions seemed to give way all at once. There have been many men of culture and more favorable surroundings who have thrown themselves away with less provocation. As it was, Bud quit school, avoided Ralph, and seemed more than ever under the influence of Dr. Small, besides becoming the intimate of Walter Johnson, Small's student and Mrs. Matilda White's son. They made a strange pair—Bud with his firm jaw and silent, cautious manner, and Walter Johnson with his weak chin, his nice neck-ties, and general dandy appearance.

To be thus deserted in his darkest hour by his only friend was the bitterest ingredient in Ralph's cup. In vain he sought an interview. Bud always eluded him. While by all the faces about him Ralph learned that the storm was getting nearer and nearer to himself. It might delay. If it had been Pete Jones alone, it might blow over. But Ralph felt sure that the relentless hand of Dr. Small was present in all his troubles. And he had only to look into Small's eye to know how inextinguishable was a malignity that burned so steadily and so quietly.

But there is no cup of unmixed bitterness. With an innocent man there is no night so dark that some star does not shine. Ralph had one strong sheet-anchor. On his return from Lewisburg on Monday Bud had handed him a note, written on common blue foolscap, in round, old-fashioned hand. It ran:

"Dear Sir: Anybody who can do so good a thing as you did for our Shocky, can not be bad. I hope you will forgive me. All the appearances in the world, and all that anybody says, can not make me think you anything else but a good man. I hope God will reward you. You must not answer this, and you hadn't better see me again, or think any more of what you spoke about the other night. I shall be a slave for three years more, and then I must work for my mother and Shocky; but I felt so bad to think that I had spoken so hard to you, that I could not help writing this. Respectfully,

"HANNAH THOMSON.

"To MR. R. HARTSOOK, ESQ."

Ralph read it over and over. What else he did with it I shall not tell. You want to know whether he kissed it, and put it into his bosom. Many a man as intelligent and manly as Hartsook has done quite as foolish a thing as that. You have been a little silly perhaps—if it is silly—and you have acted in a sentimental sort of a way over such things. But it would never do for me to tell you what Ralph did. Whether he put the letter into his bosom or not, he put the words into his heart, and, metaphorically speaking, he shook that little blue billet, written on coarse foolscap paper—he shook that little letter, full of confidence, in the face and eyes of all the calamities that haunted him. If Hannah believed in him, the whole world might distrust him. When Hannah was in one scale and the whole world in the other, of what account was the world? Justice may be blind, but all the pictures of blind cupids in the world can not make Love blind. And it was well that Ralph weighed things in this way. For the time was come in which he needed all the courage the blue billet could give him.

CHAPTER XXVIII

THE FLIGHT

ABOUT ten days after Ralph's return to Flat Creek things came to a crisis.

The master was rather relieved at first to have the crisis come. He had been holding juvenile Flat Creek under his feet by sheer force of will. And such an exercise of "psychic power" is very exhausting. In racing on the Ohio the engineer sometimes sends the largest of the firemen to hold the safety-valve down, and this he does by hanging himself to the lever by his hands. Ralph felt that he had been holding the safety-valve down, and that he was so weary of the operation that an explosion would be a real relief. He was a little tired of having everybody look on him as a thief. It was a little irksome to know that new bolts were put on the doors of the houses in which he had staid. And now that Shocky was gone, and Bud had turned against him, and Aunt Matilda suspected him, and even poor, weak, exquisite Walter Johnson would not associate with him, he felt himself an outlaw indeed. He would have gone away to Texas or the new gold fields in California had it not been for one thing. That letter on blue foolscap paper kept a little warmth in his heart.

His course from school on the evening that some-

thing happened lay through the sugar-camp. Among
the dark trunks of the maples, solemn and lofty
pillars, he debated the case. To stay, or to flee?
The worn nerves could not keep their present tension
much longer.

It was just by the brook, or, as they say in Indiana, the "branch,"[1] that something happened
which brought him to a sudden decision. Ralph
never afterward could forget that brook. It was a
swift-running little stream, that did not babble
blatantly over the stones. It ran through a thicket
of willows, through the sugar-camp, and out into
Means's pasture. Ralph had just passed through
the thicket, had just crossed the brook on the half-
decayed log that spanned it, when, as he emerged
from the water-willows on the other side, he started
with a sudden shock. For there was Hannah, with
a white, white face, holding out a little note folded
like an old-fashioned thumb-paper.

"Go quick!" she stammered as she slipped it into
Ralph's hand, inadvertently touching his fingers
with her own—a touch that went tingling through the
schoolmaster's nerves. But she had hardly said the
words until she was gone down the brookside path
and over into the pasture. A few minutes afterward

---

[1] I have already mentioned the absence of *pail* and *pare* from the ancient
Hoosier folk-speech. *Brook* is likewise absent.   The illiterate Indiana countryman before the Civil War, let us say, had no pails, pared no apples, husked no
corn, crossed no brooks. The same is true, I believe, of the South generally.
As the first settlers on the Southern coast entered the land by the rivers, each
smaller stream was regarded as a branch of the larger one. A small stream was
therefore called a *branch*. The word brook was probably lost in the first generation. But a small stream is often called a *run* in the Middle and Southern belt.
Halliwell gives *rundel* as used with the same signification in England, and he gives
ryn in the same sense from an old manuscript.

she drove the cows up into the lot and meekly took her scolding from Mrs. Means for being gone sech an awful long time, like a lazy, good-fer-nothin' piece of goods that she was.

Ralph opened the thumb-paper note, written on a page torn from an old copy-book, in Bud's "hand-write" and running:

"Mr. Heartsook
    "deer Sur:
    "i Put in my best licks, taint no use. Run fer yore life. A plans on foot to tar an fether or wuss to-night. Go rite off. Things is awful juberous.[1]
                          "Bud."

The first question with Ralph was whether he could depend on Bud. But he soon made up his mind that treachery of any sort was not one of his traits. He had mourned over the destruction of Bud's good resolutions by Martha Hawkins's refusal, and being a disinterested party he could have comforted Bud by explaining Martha's "mitten." But he felt sure that Bud was not treacherous. It was a relief, then, as he stood there to know that the false truce was over, and worst had come to worst.

His first impulse was to stay and fight. But his nerves were not strong enough to execute so fool-

---

[1] *Juberous* is in none of the vocabularies that I have seen. I once treated this word in print as an undoubted corruption of *dubious*, and when used subjectively it apparently feels the influence of dubious, as where one says: "I feel mighty juberous about it." But it is much oftener applied as in the text to the object of fear, as "The bridge looks kind o' juberous." Halliwell gives the verb *juberd* and defines it as "to jeopard or endanger." It is clearly a dialect form of *jeopard*, and I make no doubt that *juberous* is a dialect variation of *jeopardous*, occasionally used as a form of *dubious*.

hardy a resolution. He seemed to see a man behind every maple-trunk. Darkness was fast coming on, and he knew that his absence from supper at his boarding-place could not fail to excite suspicion. There was no time to be lost. So he started.

Once run from a danger, and panic is apt to ensue. The forest, the stalk-fields, the dark hollows through which he passed, seemed to be peopled with terrors. He knew Small and Jones well enough to know that every avenue of escape would be carefully picketed. So there was nothing to do but to take the shortest path to the old trysting place, the Spring-in-rock.

Here he sat and shook with terror. Angry with himself, he inly denounced himself for a coward. But the effect was really a physical one. The chill and panic now were the reaction from the previous strain.

For when the sound of his pursuers' voices broke upon his ears early in the evening, Ralph shook no more; the warm blood set back again toward the extremities, and his self-control returned when he needed it. He gathered some stones about him, as the only weapons of defense at hand. The mob was on the cliff above. But he thought that he heard footsteps in the bed of the creek below. If this were so, there could be no doubt that his hiding-place was suspected.

"O Hank!" shouted Bud from the top of the cliff to some one in the creek below, "be sure to look at the Spring-in-rock—I think he's there."

This hint was not lost on Ralph, who speedily changed his quarters by climbing up to a secluded, shelf-like ledge above the spring. He was none too soon, for Pete Jones and Hank Banta were soon looking all around the spring for him, while he held a twenty-pound stone over their heads ready to drop upon them in case they should think of looking on the ledge above.

When the crowd were gone Ralph knew that one road was open to him. He could follow down the creek to Clifty, and thence he might escape. But, traveling down to Clifty, he debated whether it was best to escape. To flee was to confess his guilt, to make himself an outlaw, to put an insurmountable barrier between himself and Hannah, whose terror-striken and anxious face as she stood by the brook-willows haunted him now, and was an involuntary witness to her love.

Long before he reached Clifty his mind was made up not to flee another mile. He knocked at the door of Squire Underwood. But Squire Underwood was also a doctor, and had been called away. He knocked at the door of Squire Doolittle. But Squire Doolittle had gone to Lewisburg. He was about to give up all hope of being able to surrender himself to the law when he met Squire Hawkins, who had come over to Clifty to avoid responsibility for the ill-deeds of his neighbors which he was powerless to prevent.

"Is that you, Mr. Hartsook?"

"Yes, and I want you to arrest me and try me here in Clifty."

CHAPTER XXIX

THE TRIAL

THE "prosecuting attorney" (for so the State's attorney is called in Indiana) had been sent for the night before. Ralph refused all legal help. It was not wise to reject counsel, but all his blood was up, and he declared that he would not be cleared by legal quibbles. If his innocence were not made evident to everybody, he would rather not be acquitted on a preliminary examination. He would go over to the circuit court and have the matter sifted to the bottom. But he would have been pleased had his uncle offered his counsel, though he would have declined it. He would have felt better to have had a letter from home somewhat different from the one he received from his Aunt Matilda by the hand of the prosecuting attorney. It was not very encouraging or very sympathetic, though it was very characteristic.

"Dear Ralph:

"This is what I have always been afraid of. I warned you faithfully the last time I saw you. My skirts are clear of your blood. I can not consent for your uncle to appear as your counsel or to go your bail. You know how much it would injure him in the county, and he has no right to suffer for your evil acts. O my dear nephew! for the sake of your poor, dead mother——"

We never shall know what the rest of that letter was. Whenever Aunt Matilda got to Ralph's poor, dead mother in her conversation Ralph ran out of the house. And now that his poor, dead mother was again made to do service in his aunt's pious rhetoric, he landed the letter on the hot coals before him, and watched it vanish into smoke with a grim satisfaction.

Ralph was a little afraid of a mob. But Clifty was better than Flat Creek, and Squire Hawkins, with all his faults, loved justice, and had a profound respect for the majesty of the law, and a profound respect for his own majesty when sitting as a court representing the law. Whatever maneuvers he might resort to in business affairs in order to avoid a conflict with his lawless neighbors, he was courageous and inflexible on the bench. The Squire was the better part of him. With the co-operation of the constable, he had organized a *posse* of men who could be depended on to enforce the law against a mob.

By the time the trial opened in the large schoolhouse in Clifty at eleven o'clock, all the surrounding country had emptied its population into Clifty, and all Flat Creek was on hand ready to testify to something. Those who knew the least appeared to know the most, and were prodigal of their significant winks and nods. Mrs. Means had always suspected him. She seed some mighty suspicious things about him from the word go. She'd allers had her doubts whether he was jist the thing, and ef her ole man had axed her, liker-n not he never'd a been hired. She'd seed things with her own livin' eyes that beat all she ever seed in all her born days. And Pete Jones said he'd allers knowed ther warn't no good in sech a feller. Couldn't stay abed when he got there. And Granny Sanders said, Law's sakes! nobody'd ever a found him out ef it hadn't been fer her. Didn't she go all over the neighborhood a-warnin' people? Fer her part, she seed straight through that piece of goods. He was fond of the gals, too! Nothing was so great a crime in her eyes as to be fond of the gals.

The constable paid unwitting tribute to William the Conquerer by crying Squire Hawkins's court open with an Oyez! or, as he said, "O yes!" and the Squire asked Squire Underwood, who came in at that minute, to sit with him. From the start, it was evident to Ralph that the prosecuting attorney had been thoroughly posted by Small, though, looking at that worthy's face, one would have thought him the most disinterested and philosophical spectator in the court-room.

Bronson, the prosecutor, was a young man, and this was his first case since his election. He was very ambitious to distinguish himself, very anxious to have Flat Creek influence on his side in politics; and, consequently, he was very determined to send Ralph Hartsook to State prison, justly or unjustly, by fair means or foul. To his professional eyes this was not a question of right and wrong, not a question of life or death to such a man as Ralph. It was

George H. Bronson's opportunity to distinguish himself. And so, with many knowing and confident nods and hints, and with much deference to the two squires, he opened the case, affecting great indignation at Ralph's wickedness, and uttering Delphic hints about striped pants and shaven head, and the grating of prison-doors at Jeffersonville.

"And, now, if the court please, I am about to call a witness whose testimony is very important indeed. Mrs. Sarah Jane Means will please step forward and be sworn."

This Mrs. Means did with alacrity. She had met the prosecutor, and impressed him with her dark hints. She was sworn.

"Now, Mrs. Means, have the goodness to tell us what you know of the robbery at the house of Peter Schroeder, and the part defendant had in it."

"Well, you see, I allers suspected that air young man——"

Here Squire Underwood stopped her, and told her that she must not tell her suspicions, but facts.

"Well, it's facts I am a-going to tell," she sniffed indignantly. "It's facts that I mean to tell." Here her voice rose to a keen pitch, and she began to abuse the defendant. Again and again the court insisted that she must tell what there was suspicious about the schoolmaster. At last she got it out.

"Well, fer one thing, what kind of gals did he go with? Hey? Why, with my bound gal, Hanner, a-loafin' along through the blue-grass paster at ten o'clock, and keepin' that gal that's got no protector but me out that a-way, and destroyin' her character by his company, that a'n't fit fer nobody."

Here Bronson saw that he had caught a tartar. He said he had no more questions to ask of Mrs. Means, and that, unless the defendant wished to cross-question her, she could stand aside. Ralph said he would like to ask her one question.

"Did I ever go with your daughter Miranda?"

"No, you didn't," answered the witness, with a tone and a toss of the head that let the cat out, and set the court-room in a giggle. Bronson saw that he was gaining nothing, and now resolved to follow the line which Small had indicated.

Pete Jones was called, and swore point-blank that he heard Ralph go out of the house soon after he went to bed, and that he heard him return at two in the morning. This testimony was given without hestitation, and made a great impression against Ralph in the minds of the justices. Mrs. Jones, a poor, brow-beaten woman, came on the stand in a frightened way, and swore to the same lies as her husband. Ralph cross-questioned her, but her part had been well learned.

There seemed now little hope for Ralph. But just as this moment who should stride into the schoolhouse but Pearson, the one-legged old soldier basket-maker? He had crept home the night before, "to see ef the ole woman didn't want somethin'," and hearing of Ralph's arrest, he concluded that the time for him to make "a forrard movement" had come, and so he determined to face the foe.

"Looky here, Squar," he said, wiping the perspiration from his brow, "looky here. I jes want to say that I kin tell as much about this case as anybody."

"Let us hear it, then," said Bronson, who thought he would nail Ralph now for certain.

So, with many allusions to the time he fit at Lundy's Lane, and some indignant remarks about the pack of thieves that driv him off, and a passing tribute to Miss Martha Hawkins, and sundry other digressions, in which he had to be checked, the old man told how he'd drunk whisky at Welch's store that night, and how Welch's whisky was all-fired mean, and how it allers went straight to his head, and how he had got a leetle too much, and how he had felt kyinder gin aout by the time he got to the blacksmith's shop, and how he had laid down to rest, and how as he s'posed the boys had crated him, and how he thought it war all-fired mean to crate a old soldier what fit the Britishers, and lost his leg by one of the blamed critters a-punchin' his bago-net[1] through it; and how when he woke up it was all-fired cold, and how he rolled off the crate and went on to*wurds* home, and how when he got up to the top of Means's hill he met Pete Jones and Bill Jones, and a slim sort of a young man, a-ridin'; and how he know'd the Joneses by ther hosses, and some more things of that kyind about 'em; but he didn't know the slim young man, tho' he tho't he

---

[1] This form, *bagonet*, is not in the vocabularies, but it was spoken as I have written it. The Century Dictionary gives *bagnet*, and Halliwell and Wright both give *baginet* with the *g* soft apparently, though neither the one nor the other is very explicit in distinguishing transcriptions from old authors from phonetic spellings of dialect forms. I fancy that this *bagonet* is impossible as a corruption of *bayonet*, and that it points to some other derivation of that word than the doubtful one from *Bayonne*.

might tell him ef he seed him agin kase he was
dressed up so slick and town-like. But blamed ef
he didn't think it hard that a passel of thieves sech
as the Joneses should try to put ther mean things
on to a man like the master, that was so kyind to
him and to Shocky, tho', fer that matter, blamed
ef he didn't think we was all selfish, akordin' to his
tell. Had seed somebody that night a-crossin' over
the blue-grass paster. Didn't know who in thunder
'twas, but it was somebody a-makin' straight fer
Pete Jones's. Hadn't seed nobody else, 'ceptin' Dr.
Small, a short ways behind the Joneses.

Hannah was now brought on the stand. She
was greatly agitated, and answered with much re-
luctance. Lived at Mr. Means's. Was eighteen
years of age in October. Had been bound to Mrs.
Means three years ago. Had walked home with
Mr. Hartsook that evening, and, happening to look
out of the window toward morning, she saw some
one cross the pasture. Did not know who it was.
Thought it was Mr. Hartsook. Here Mr. Bronson
(evidently prompted by a suggestion that came
from what Small had overheard when he listened
in the barn) asked her if Mr. Hartsook had ever
said anything to her about the matter afterward.
After some hesitation, Hannah said that he had
said that he crossed the pasture. Of his own accord?
No, she spoke of it first. Had Mr. Hartsook offered
any explanations? No, he hadn't. Had he ever paid
her any attention afterward? No. Ralph declined
to cross-question Hannah. To him she never seemed
so fair as when telling the truth so sublimely.

Bronson now informed the court that this little trick of having the old soldier happen in, in the nick of time, wouldn't save the prisoner at the bar from the just punishment which an outraged law visited upon such crimes as his. He regretted that his duty as a public prosecutor caused it to fall to his lot to marshal the evidence that was to blight the prospects and blast the character, and annihilate for ever, so able and promising a young man, but that the law knew no difference between the educated and the uneducated, and that for his part he thought Hartsook a most dangerous foe to the peace of society. The evidence already given fastened suspicion upon him. The prisoner had not yet been able to break its force at all. The prisoner had not even dared to try to explain to a young lady the reason for his being out at night. He would now conclude by giving the last touch to the dark evidence that would sink the once fair name of Ralph Hartsook in a hundred fathoms of infamy. He would ask that Henry Banta be called.

Hank came forward sheepishly, and was sworn. Lived about a hundred yards from the house that was robbed. He seen ole man Pearson and the master and one other feller that he didn't know come away from there together about one o'clock. He heerd the horses kickin', and went out to the stable to see about them. He seed two men come out of Schroeder's back door and meet one man standing at the gate. When they got closter he knowed Pearson by his wooden leg and the master by his hat. On cross-examination he was a little confused when asked why he hadn't told of it before, but said that he was afraid to say much, bekase the folks was a-talkin' about hanging the master, and he didn't want no lynchin'.

The prosecution here rested, Bronson maintaining that there was enough evidence to justify Ralph's committal to await trial. But the court thought that as the defendant had no counsel and offered no rebutting testimony, it would be only fair to hear what the prisoner had to say in his own defense.

All this while poor Ralph was looking about the room for Bud. Bud's actions had of late been strangely contradictory. But had he turned coward and deserted his friend? Why else did he avoid the session of the court? After asking himself such questions as these, Ralph would wonder at his own folly. What could Bud do if he were there? There was no human power that could prevent the victim of so vile a conspiracy as this, lodging in that worst of State prisons at Jeffersonville, a place too bad for criminals. But when there is no human power to help, how naturally does the human mind look for some divine intervention on the side of Right! And Ralph's faith in Providence looked in the direction of Bud. But since no Bud came, he shut down the valves and rose to his feet, proudly, defiantly, fiercely calm.

"It's of no use for me to say anything. Peter Jones has sworn to a deliberate falsehood, and he knows it. He has made his wife perjure her poor soul that she dare not call her own." Here Pete's fists clenched, but Ralph in his present humor did not care for mobs. The spirit of the bulldog had complete possession of him. "It is of no use for me to tell you that Henry Banta has sworn to a lie, partly to revenge himself on me for punishments I have given him, and partly, perhaps, for money. The real thieves are in this court-room. I could put my finger on them."

"*To* be sure," responded the old basket-maker. Ralph looked at Pete Jones, then at Small. The fiercely calm look attracted the attention of the people. He knew that this look would probably cost him his life before the next morning. But he did not care for life. "The testimony of Miss Hannah Thomson is every word true. I believe that of Mr. Pearson to be true. The rest is false. But I can not prove it. I know the men I have to deal with. I shall not escape with State prison. They will not spare my life. But the people of Clifty will one day find out who are the thieves." Ralph then proceeded to tell how he had left Pete Jones's, Mr. Jones's bed being uncomfortable; how he had walked through the pasture; how he had seen three men on horseback; how he had noticed the sorrel with the white left forefoot and white nose; how he had seen Dr. Small; how, after his return, he had heard some one enter the house, and how he had recognized the horse the next morning. "There," said Ralph desperately, leveling his finger at Pete, "there is a man who will yet see the inside of a penitentiary. I shall not live to see it, but the rest of you will." Pete quailed. Ralph's speech could not of course break the force of the testimony against him.   But it had its effect, and it had effect enough to alarm Bronson, who rose and said:

"I should like to ask the prisoner at the bar one question."

"Ask me a dozen," said Hartsook, looking more like a king than a criminal.

"Well, then, Mr. Hartsook.   You need not answer unless you choose; but what prompted you to take the direction you did in your walk on that evening?"

This shot brought Ralph down.   To answer this question truly would attach to friendless Hannah Thomson some of the disgrace that now belonged to him.

"I decline to answer," said Ralph.

"Of course, I do not want the prisoner to criminate himself," said Bronson significantly.

During this last passage Bud had come in, but, to Ralph's disappointment he remained near the door, talking to Walter Johnson, who had come with him.   The magistrates put their heads together to fix the amount of bail, and, as they differed, talked for some minutes.   Small now for the first time thought best to make a move in his own proper person.   He could hardly have been afraid of Ralph's acquittal.   He may have been a little anxious at the manner in which he had been mentioned, and at the significant look of Ralph, and he probably meant to excite indignation enough against the schoolmaster to break the force of his speech, and secure the lynching of the prisoner, chiefly by people outside his gang.   He rose and asked the court in gentlest tones to hear him.   He had no personal

interest in this trial, except his interest in the wel-
fare of his old schoolmate, Mr. Hartsook. He was
grieved and disappointed to find the evidence
against him so damaging and he would not for the
world add a feather to it, if it were not that his own
name had been twice alluded to by the defendant, and
by his friend, and perhaps his confederate, John
Pearson. He was prepared to swear that he was not
over in Flat Creek the night of the robbery later
than ten o'clock, and while the statements of the
two persons alluded to, whether maliciously intended or not, could not implicate him at all, he
thought perhaps this lack of veracity in their statements might be of weight in determining some
other points. He therefore suggested—he could
only suggest, as he was not a party to the case in
any way—that his student, Mr. Walter Johnson, be
called to testify as to his—Dr. Small's—exact
whereabouts on the night in question. They were
together in his office until two, when he went to the
tavern and went to bed.

Squire Hawkins, having adjusted his teeth, his
wig, and his glass eye, thanked Dr. Small for a suggestion so valuable, and thought best to put John
Pearson under arrest before proceeding further. Mr.
Pearson was therefore arrested, and was heard to
mutter something about a "passel of thieves," when
the court warned him to be quiet.

Walter Johnson was then called. But before giving
his testimony, I must crave the reader's patience while
I go back to some things which happened nearly a
week before and which will serve to make it intelligible.

CHAPTER XXX

"BROTHER SODOM"

In order to explain Walter Johnson's testimony and his state of mind, I must carry the reader back nearly a week. The scene was Dr. Small's office. Bud and Walter Johnson had been having some confidential conversation that evening, and Bud had got more out of his companion than that exquisite but weak young man had intended. He looked round in a frightened way.

"You see," said Walter, "if Small knew I had told you that, I'd get a bullet some night from somebody. But when you're initiated it'll be all right. Sometimes I wish I was out of it. But, you know, Small's this kind of a man. He sees through you. He can look through a door"—and there he shivered, and his voice broke down into a whisper. But Bud was perfectly cool, and doubtless it was the strong coolness of Bud that made Walter, who shuddered at a shadow, come to him for sympathy and unbosom himself of one of his guilty secrets.

"Let's go and hear Brother Sodom preach to-night," said Bud.

"No, I don't like to."

"He don't scare you?" There was just a touch of ridicule in Bud's voice. He knew Walter, and he had not counted amiss when he used this little goad

to prick a skin so sensitive. "Brother Sodom" was
the nickname given by scoffers to the preacher—
Mr. Soden—whose manner of preaching had so
aroused Bud's combativeness, and whose saddle-
stirrups Bud had helped to amputate. For reasons
of his own, Bud thought best to subject young
Johnson to the heat of Mr. Soden's furnace.

Peter Cartwright boasts that, on a certain occasion, he "shook his brimstone wallet" over the
people. Mr. Soden could never preach without his
brimstone wallet. There are those of refinement so
attenuated that they will not admit that fear can
have any place in religion. But a religion without
fear could never have evangelized or civilized the
West, which at one time bade fair to become a
perdition as bad as any that Brother Sodom ever
depicted. And against these on the one side, and
the Brother Sodoms on the other, I shall interrupt
my story to put this chapter under shelter of that
wise remark of the great Dr. Adam Clark, who says
"The fear of God is the beginning of wisdom, the
terror of God confounds the soul;" and that other
saying of his: "With the *fear* of God the love of
God is ever consistent; but where the *terror* of the
Lord reigns, there can neither be *fear*, *faith*, nor
love; nay, nor *hope* either." And yet I am not sure
that even the Brother Sodoms were made in vain.

On this evening Mr. Soden was as terrible as
usual. Bud heard him without flinching. Small,
who sat farther forward, listened with pious approval. Mr. Soden, out of distorted figures pieced
together from different passages of Scripture, built

a hell, not quite Miltonic, nor yet Dantean, but as Miltonic and Dantean as his unrefined imagination could make it. As he rose toward his climax of hideous description, Walter Johnson trembled from head to foot and sat close to Bud. Then, as burly Mr. Soden, with great gusto, depicted materialistic tortures that startled the nerves of everybody except Bud, Walter wanted to leave, but Bud would not let him. For some reason he wished to keep his companion in the crucible as long as possible.

"Young man!" cried Mr. Soden, and the explosive voice seemed to come from the hell that he had created—"young man! you who have followed the counsel of evil companions"—here he paused and looked about, as if trying to find the man he wanted, while Walter crept up close to Bud and shaded his face—"I mean you who have chosen evil pursuits and who can not get free from bad habits and associations that are dragging you down to hell! You are standing on the very crumbling brink of hell to-night. The smell of the brimstone is on your garments, the hot breath of hell is in your face! The devils are waiting for you! Delay and you are damned! You may die before daylight! You may never get out that door! The awful angel of death is just ready to strike you down!" Here some shrieked with terror, others sobbed, and Brother Sodom looked with approval on the storm he had awakened. The very harshness of his tone, his lofty egotism of manner, that which had roused all Bud's combativeness, shook poor Walter as a wind would shake a reed. In the midst of the general excitement he seized his hat and hastened out the door. Bud followed, while Soden shot his lightnings after them, declaring that "young men who ran away from the truth would dwell in torments forever."

Bud had not counted amiss when he thought that Mr. Soden's preaching would be likely to arouse so mean-spirited a fellow as Walter. So vivid was the impression that Johnson begged Bud to return to the office with him. He felt sick, and was afraid that he should die before morning. He insisted that Bud should stay with him all night. To this Means readily consented, and by morning he had heard all that the frightened Walter had to tell.

And now let us return to the trial, where Ralph sits waiting the testimony of Walter Johnson, which is to prove his statement false.

CHAPTER XXXI

THE TRIAL CONCLUDED

I DO not know how much interest the "gentle reader" may feel in Bud. But I venture to hope that there are some Buddhists among my readers who will wish the contradictoriness of his actions explained. The first dash of disappointment had well-nigh upset him. And when a man concludes to throw overboard his good resolutions, he always seeks to avoid the witness of those resolutions. Hence Bud, after that distressful Tuesday evening on which Miss Martha had given him "the sack," wished to see Ralph less than any one else. And yet when he came to suspect Small's villainy, his whole nature revolted at it. But having broken with Ralph, he thought it best to maintain an attitude of apparent hostility, that he might act as a detective, and, perhaps, save his friend from the mischief that threatened him. As soon as he heard of Ralph's arrest he determined to make Walter Johnson tell his own secret in court, because he knew that it would be best for Ralph that Walter should tell it. Bud's telling at second-hand would not be conclusive. And he sincerely desired to save Walter from prison. For Walter Johnson was the victim of Dr. Small, or of Dr. Small and such novels as "The Pirate's Bride," "Claude Duval," "The Wild Rover of the

West Indies," and the cheap biographies of such
men as Murrell. Small found him with his imagination inflamed by the history of such heroes, and
opened to him the path to glory for which he
longed.

The whole morning after Ralph's arrest Bud was
working on Walter's conscience and his fears. The
poor fellow, unable to act for himself, was torn
asunder between the old ascendency of Small and
the new ascendency of Bud Means. Bud finally
frightened him, by the fear of the penitentiary, into
going to the place of trial. But once inside the door,
and once in sight of Small, who was more to him
than God, or, rather, more to him than the devil—
for the devil was Walter's God, or, perhaps, I
should say, Walter's God was a devil—once in
sight of Small, he refused to move an inch farther.
And Bud, after all his perseverance, was about to
give up in sheer despair.

Fortunately, just at that moment Small's desire
to relieve himself from the taint of suspicion and
to crush Ralph as completely as possible, made him
overshoot the mark by asking that Walter be called
to the stand, as we have before recounted. He
knew that he had no tool so supple as the cowardly
Walter. In the very language of the request, he
had given Walter an intimation of what he wanted
him to swear to. Walter listened to Small's words
as to his doom. He felt that he should die of inde-
cision. The perdition of a man of his stamp is to
have to make up his mind. Such men generally
fall back on some one more positive, and take all

their resolutions ready-made. But here Walter must decide for himself. For the constable was already calling his name; the court, the spectators, and, most of all, Dr. Small, were waiting for him. He moved forward mechanically through the dense crowd, Bud following part of the way to whisper, "Tell the truth or go to penitentiary." Walter shook and shivered at this. The witness with difficulty held up his hand long enough to be sworn.

"Please tell the court," said Bronson, "whether you know anything of the whereabouts of Dr. Small on the night of the robbery at Peter Schroeder's."

Small had detected Walter's agitation, and, taking alarm, had edged his way around so as to stand full in Walter's sight, and there, with keen, magnetic eye on the weak orbs of the young man, he was able to assume his old position, and sway the fellow absolutely.

"On the night of the robbery"—Walter's voice was weak, but he seemed to be reading his answer out of Small's eyes—"on the night of the robbery Dr. Small came home before——" here the witness stopped and shook and shivered again. For Bud, detecting the effect of Small's gaze, had pushed his great hulk in front of Small, and had fastened his eyes on Walter with a look that said. "Tell the truth or go to penitentiary."

"I can't, I can't. O God! What shall I do?" the witness exclaimed, answering the look of Bud. For it seemed to him that Bud had spoken. To the people and the court this agitation was inexplicable. Squire Hawkins's wig got awry, his glass eye turned in toward his nose, and he had great difficulty in keeping his teeth from falling out. The excitement became painfully intense. Ralph was on his feet, looking at the witness, and feeling that somehow Bud and Dr. Small—his good angel and his demon—were playing an awful game, of which he was the stake. The crowd swayed to and fro, but remained utterly silent, waiting to hear the least whisper from the witness, who stood trembling a moment with his hands over his face, and then fainted.

The fainting of a person in a crowd is a signal for everybody else to make fools of themselves. There was a rush toward the fainting man, there was a cry for water. Everybody asked everybody else to open the window, and everybody wished everybody else to stand back and give him air. But nobody opened the window, and nobody stood back. The only perfectly cool man in the room was Small. With a quiet air of professional authority he pushed forward and felt the patient's pulse, remarking to the court that he thought it was a sudden attack of fever with delirium. When Walter revived, Dr. Small would have removed him, but Ralph insisted that his testimony should be heard. Under pretense of watching his patient, Small kept close to him. And Walter began the same old story about Dr. Small's having arrived at the office before eleven o'clock, when Bud came up behind the doctor and fastened his eyes on the witness with the same significant look, and Walter, with visions of the penitentiary before him halted, stammered, and seemed about to faint again.

"If the court please," said Bronson, "this witness is evidently intimidated by that stout young man," pointing to Bud. "I have seen him twice interrupt witness's testimony by casting threatening looks at him. I trust the court will have him removed from the court-room."

After a few moments' consultation, during which Squire Hawkins held his wig in place with one hand and alternately adjusted his eye and his spectacles with the other, the magistrates, who were utterly bewildered by the turn things were taking, decided that it could do no harm, and that it was best to try the experiment of removing Bud. Perhaps Johnson would then be able to get through with his testimony. The constable therefore asked Bud if he would please leave the room. Bud cast one last look at the witness and walked out like a captive bear.

Ralph stood watching the receding form of Bud. The emergency had made him as cool as Small ever was. Bud stopped at the door, where he was completely out of sight of the witness, concealed by the excited spectators, who stood on the benches to see what was going on in front.

"The witness will please proceed," said Bronson.

"If the court please"—it was Ralph who spoke —"I believe I have as much at stake in this trial as any one. That witness is evidently intimidated. But not by Mr. Means. I ask that Dr. Small be removed out of sight of the witness."

"A most extraordinary request, truly." This was what Small's bland countenance said; he did not open his lips.

"It's no more than fair," said Squire Hawkins, adjusting his wig, "that the witness be relieved of everything that anybody might think affects his veracity in this matter."

Dr. Small, giving Walter one friendly, appealing look, moved back by the door, and stood alongside Bud, as meek, quiet, and disinterested as any man in the house.

"The witness will now proceed with his testimony." This time it was Squire Hawkins who spoke. Bronson had been attacked with a suspicion that this witness was not just what he wanted, and had relapsed into silence.

Walter's struggle was by no means ended by the disappearance of Small and Bud. There came the recollection of his mother's stern face—a face which had never been a motive toward the right, but only a goad to deception. What would she say if he should confess? Just as he had recovered himself, and was about to repeat the old lie which had twice died upon his lips at the sight of Bud's look, he caught sight of another face, which made him tremble again. It was the lofty and terrible countenance of Mr. Soden. One might have thought, from the expression it wore, that the seven last vials were in his hands, the seven apocalyptic trumpets waiting for his lips, and the seven thunders sitting upon his eyebrows. The moment that Walter saw him he smelled the brimstone on his own garments, he felt himself upon the crumbling brink of the precipice, with perdition below him. Now I am sure that "Brother Sodoms" were not made wholly in vain. There are plenty of mean-spirited men like Walter Johnson, whose feeble consciences need all the support they can get from the fear of perdition, and who are incapable of any other conception of it than a coarse and materialistic one. Let us set it down to the credit of Brother Sodom, with his stiff stock, his thunderous face, and his awful walk, that his influence over Walter was on the side of truth.

"Please proceed," said Squire Hawkins to Walter. The Squire's wig lay on one side, he had forgotten to adjust his eye, and he leaned forward, tremulous with interest.

"Well, then," said Walter, looking not at the court nor at Bronson nor at the prisoner, but furtively at Mr. Soden—"well, then, if I must"—and Mr. Soden's awful face seemed to answer that he surely must—"well, then, I hope you won't send me to prison"—this to Squire Hawkins, whose face reassured him—"but, oh! I don't see how I can!" But one look at Mr. Soden assured him that he could and that he must, and so, with an agony painful to the spectators, he told the story in driblets. How, while yet in Lewisburg, he had been made a member of a gang of which Small was chief; how they concealed from him the names of all the band except six, of whom the Joneses and Small were three.

Here there was a scuffle at the door. The court demanded silence.

"Dr. Small's trying to git out, plague take him," said Bud, who stood with his back planted against the door. "I'd like the court to send and git his trunk afore he has a chance to burn up all the papers that's in it."

"Constable, you will arrest Dr. Small, Peter Jones, and William Jones. Send two deputies to bring Small's trunk into court," said Squire Underwood.

The prosecuting attorney was silent.

Walter then told of the robbery at Schroeder's, told where he and Small had whittled the fence while the Joneses entered the house, and confirmed Ralph's story by telling how they had seen Ralph in a fence-corner, and how they had met the basket-maker on the hill.

"*To* be sure," said the old man, who had not ventured to hold up his head, after he was arrested, until Walter began his testimony.

Walter felt inclined to stop, but he could not do it, for there stood Mr. Soden, looking to him like a messenger from the skies, or the bottomless pit, sent to extort the last word from his guilty soul. He felt that he was making a clean breast of it—at the risk of perdition, with the penitentiary thrown in, if he faltered. And so he told the whole thing as though it had been the day of doom, and by the time he was through, Small's trunk was in court.

Here a new hubbub took place at the door. It was none other than the crazy pauper, Tom Bifield, who personated General Andrew Jackson in the poor-house. He had caught some inkling of the trial, and had escaped in Bill Jones's absence. His red plume was flying, and in his tattered and filthy garb he was indeed a picturesque figure.

"Squar," said he, elbowing his way through the crowd, "I kin tell you somethin'. I'm Gineral Andrew Jackson. Lost my head at Bueny Visty. This head growed on. It a'n't good fer much. One side's tater. But t'other's sound as a nut. Now, I kin give you information."

Bronson, with the quick perceptions of a politician, had begun to see which way future winds would probably blow. "If the court please," he said, "this man is not wholly sane, but we might get valuable information out of him. I suggest that his testimony be taken for what it is worth."

"No, you don't swar me," broke in the lunatic. "Not if I knows myself. You see, when a feller's got one side of his head tater, he's mighty onsartain like. You don't swar me, fer I can't tell what minute the tater side'll begin to talk. I'm talkin' out of the lef' side now, and I'm all right. But you don't swar me. But ef you'll send some of your constables out to the barn at the pore-house and look under the hay-mow in the north-east corner, you'll find some things maybe as has been a-missin' fer some time. And that a'n't out of the tater side, nuther."

Meantime Bud did not rest. Hearing the nature of the testimony given by Hank Banta before he entered, he attacked Hank and vowed he'd send him to prison if he didn't make a clean breast. Hank was a thorough coward—and now that his friends were prisoners, was ready enough to tell the truth if he could be protected from prosecution.

Seeing the disposition of the prosecuting attorney, Bud got from him a promise that he would do what he could to protect Hank. That worthy then took the stand, confessed his lie, and even told the inducement which Mr. Pete Jones had offered him to perjure himself.

" *To* be sure," said Pearson.

Squire Hawkins, turning his right eye upon him, while the left looked at the ceiling, said: "Be careful, Mr. Pearson, or I shall have to punish you for contempt."

"Why, Squar, I didn't know 'twas any sin to hev a healthy contemp' fer sech a thief as Jones!"

The Squire looked at Mr. Pearson severely, and the latter, feeling that he had committed some offense without knowing it, subsided into silence.

Bronson now had a keen sense of the direction of the gale.

"If the court please," said he, "I have tried to do my duty in this case. It was my duty to prosecute Mr. Hartsook, however much I might feel assured that he was innocent, and that he would be able to prove his innocence. I now enter a *nolle* in his case and that of John Pearson, and I ask that this court adjourn until to-morrow, in order to give me time to examine the evidence in the case of the other parties under arrest. I am proud to think that my efforts have been the means of sifting the matter to the bottom, of freeing Mr. Hartsook from suspicion, and of detecting the real criminals."

"Ugh!" said Mr. Pearson, who conceived a great dislike to Bronson.

"The court," said Squire Hawkins, "congratulates Mr. Hartsook on his triumphant acquittal. He is discharged from the bar of this court, and from the bar of public sentiment, without a suspicion of guilt. Constable, discharge Ralph Hartsook and John Pearson."

Old Jack Means, who had always had a warm side for the master, now proposed three cheers for Mr. Hartsook, and they were given with a will by the people who would have hanged him an hour before.

Mrs. Means gave it as her opinion that "Jack Means allers wuz a fool!"

"This court," said Dr. Underwood, "has one other duty to perform before adjourning for the day. Recall Hannah Thomson."

"I jist started her on ahead to git supper and milk the cows," said Mrs. Means. "A'n't a-goin' to have her loafin' here all day."

"Constable, recall her. This court can not adjourn until she returns!"

Hannah had gone but a little way, and was soon in the presence of the court, trembling for fear of some new calamity.

"Hannah Thomson"—it was Squire Underwood who spoke—"Hannah Thomson, this court wishes to ask you one or two questions."

"Yes, sir," but her voice died to a whisper.

"How old did you say you were?"

"Eighteen, sir, last October."

"Can you prove your age?"

"Yes, sir—by my mother."

"For how long are you bound to Mr. Means?"

"Till I'm twenty-one."

"This court feels in duty bound to inform you that, according to the laws of Indiana, a woman is of age at eighteen, and as no indenture could be made binding after you had reached your majority, you are the victim of a deception. You are free, and if it can be proven that you have been defrauded by a willful deception, a suit for damages will lie."

"Ugh!" said Mrs. Means. "You're a purty court, a'n't you, Dr. Underwood?"

"Be careful, Mrs. Means, or I shall have to fine you for contempt of court."

But the people, who were in the cheering humor, cheered Hannah and the justices, and then cheered Ralph again. Granny Sanders shook hands with him, and allers knowed he'd come out right. It allers 'peared like as if Dr. Small warn't jist the sort to tie to, you know. And old John Pearson went home, after drinking two or three glasses of Welch's whisky, keeping time to an imaginary triumphal march, and feeling prouder than he had ever felt since he fit the Britishers under Scott at Lundy's Lane. He told his wife that the master had jist knocked the hind-sights offen that air young lawyer from Lewisburg.

Walter was held to bail that he might appear as a witness, and Ralph might have sent his aunt a Roland for an Oliver. But he only sent a note to his uncle, asking him to go Walter's bail. If he had been resentful, he could not have wished for a more complete revenge than the day had brought.

CHAPTER XXXII

AFTER THE BATTLE

Nothing can be more demoralizing in the long run than lynch law. And yet lynch law often originates in a burst of generous indignation which is not willing to suffer a bold oppressor to escape by means of corrupt and cowardly courts. It is oftener born of fear. Both motives powerfully agitated the people of the region round about Clifty as night drew on after Ralph's acquittal. They were justly indignant that Ralph had been made the victim of such a conspiracy, and they were frightened at the unseen danger to the community from such a band as that of Small's. It was certain that they did not know the full extent of the danger as yet. And what Small might do with a jury, or what Pete Jones might do with a sheriff, was a question. I must not detain the reader to tell how the mob rose. Nobody knows how such things come about. Their origin is as inexplicable as that of an earthquake. But, at any rate, a rope was twice put round Small's neck during that night, and both times Small was saved only by the nerve and address of Ralph, who had learned how unjust mob law may be. As for Small, he neither trembled when they were ready to hang him, nor looked relieved when he was saved, nor showed the slightest flush of penitence or gratitude.

He bore himself in a quiet, gentlemanly way through-out, like the admirable villain that he was.

He waived a preliminary examination the next day; his father went his bail, and he forfeited bail and disappeared from the county and from the horizon of my story. Two reports concerning Small have been in circulation—one that he was running a faro-bank in San Francisco, the other that he was curing consumption in New York by some quack process. If this latter were true, it would leave it an open question whether Ralph did well to save him from the gallows. Pete Jones and Bill, as usually happens to the rougher villains, went to prison, and when their terms had expired moved to Pike County, Missouri.

But it is about Hannah that you wish to hear, and that I wish to tell. She went straight from the court-room to Flat Creek, climbed to her chamber, packed in a handkerchief all her earthly goods, con-sisting chiefly of a few family relics, and turned her back on the house of Means forever. At the gate she met the old woman, who shook her fist in the girl's face and gave her a parting benediction in the words: "You mis'able, ongrateful critter you, go 'long. I'm glad to be shed of you!" At the barn she met Bud, and he told her good-by with a little huskiness in his voice, while a tear glistened in her eyes. Bud had been a friend in need, and such a friend one does not leave without a pang.

"Where are you going? Can I——"

"No, no!" And with that she hastened on, afraid that Bud would offer to hitch up the roan colt.

And she did not want to add to his domestic un-happiness by compromising him in that way.

It was dusk and was raining when she left. The hours were long, the road was lonely, and after the revelations of that day it did not seem wholly safe. But from the moment that she found herself free, her heart had been ready to break with an impatient homesickness. What though there might be robbers in the woods? What though there were ten rough miles to travel? What though the rain was in her face? What though she had not tasted food since the morning of that exciting day? Flat Creek and bondage were behind; freedom, mother, Shocky, and home were before her, and her feet grew lighter with the thought. And if she needed any other joy, it was to know that the master was clear. And he would come? And so she traversed the weary dis-tance, and so she inquired and found the house, the beautiful, homely old house of beautiful, homely old Nancy Sawyer, and knocked, and was admitted, and fell down, faint and weary, at her blind mother's feet, and laid her tired head in her mother's lap and wept and wept like a child, and said, "O mother! I'm free! I'm free!" while the mother's tears bap-tized her face, and the mother's trembling fingers combed out her tresses. And Shocky stood by her and cried: "I knowed God wouldn't forget you, Hanner!"

Hannah was ready now to do anything by which she could support her mother and Shocky. She was strong and inured to toil. She was willing and cheerful, and she would gladly have gone to service if by that means she could have supported the family. And, for that matter her mother was already able nearly to support herself by her knitting. But Hannah had been carefully educated when young, and at that moment the old public schools were being organized into a graded school, and the good minister, who shall be nameless, because he is, perhaps, still living in Indiana, and who in Methodist parlance was called "the preacher-in-charge of Lewisburg Station"—this good minister and Miss Nancy Sawyer got Hannah a place as teacher in the primary department. And then a little house with four rooms was rented, and a little, a very little furniture was put into it, and the old, sweet home was established again. The father was gone, never to come back again. But the rest were here. And somehow Hannah kept waiting for somebody else to come.

CHAPTER XXXIII

INTO THE LIGHT

For two weeks longer Ralph taught at the Flat Creek schoolhouse. He was everybody's hero. And he was Bud's idol. He did what he could to get Bud and Martha together, and though Bud always "saw her safe home" after this, and called on her every Sunday evening, yet, to save his life, he could not forget his big fists and his big feet long enough to say what he most wanted to say, and what Martha most wanted him to say.

At the end of two weeks Ralph found himself exceedingly weary of Flat Creek, and exceedingly glad to hear from Mr. Means that the school-money had "gin out." It gave him a good excuse to return to Lewisburg, where his heart and his treasure were. A certain sense of delicacy had kept him from writing to Hannah just yet.

When he got to Lewisburg he had good news. His uncle, ashamed of his previous neglect, and perhaps with an eye to his nephew's growing popularity, had got him the charge of the grammar department in the new graded school in the village. So he quietly arranged to board at a boarding-house. His aunt could not have him about, of which fact he was very glad. She could not but feel, she said, that he might have taken better care of Walter than he did, when they were only four miles apart.

He did not hasten to call on Hannah. Why should he? He sent her a message, of no consequence in itself, by Nancy Sawyer. Then he took possession of his school; and then, on the evening of the first day of school, he went, as he had appointed to himself, to see Hannah Thomson.

And she, with some sweet presentiment, had got things ready by fixing up the scantily-furnished room as well as she could. And Miss Nancy Sawyer, who had seen Ralph that afternoon, had guessed that he was going to see Hannah. It's wonderful how much enjoyment a generous heart can get out of the happiness of others. Is not that what He meant when He said of such as Miss Sawyer that they should have a hundred-fold in this life for all their sacrifices? Did not Miss Nancy enjoy a hundred weddings and have the love of five hundred children? And so Miss Nancy just happened over at Mrs. Thomson's humble home, and, just in the most matter-of-course way, asked that lady and Shocky to come over to her house. Shocky wanted Hannah to come too. But Hannah blushed a little, and said that she would rather not.

And when she was left alone, Hannah fixed her hair two or three times, and swept the hearth, and moved the chairs first one way and then another, and did a good many other needless things. Needless: for a lover, if he be a lover, does not see furniture or dress.

And then she sat down by the fire, and tried to sew, and tried to look unconcerned, and tried to feel unconcerned, and tried not to expect anybody, and tried to make her heart keep still. And tried in vain.

For a gentle rap at the door sent her pulse up twenty beats a minute and made her face burn. And Hartsook was for the first time, abashed in the presence of Hannah. For the oppressed girl had, in two weeks, blossomed out into the full-blown woman.

And Ralph sat down by the fire, and talked of his school and her school, and everything else but what he wanted to talk about. And then the conversation drifted back to Flat Creek, and to the walk through the pasture, and to the box-elder tree, and to the painful talk in the lane. And Hannah begged to be forgiven, and Ralph laughed at the idea that she had done anything wrong. And she praised his goodness to Shocky, and he drew her little note out of—— But I agreed not tell you where he kept it. And then she blushed, and he told how the note had sustained him, and how her white face kept up his courage in his flight down the bed of Clifty Creek. And he sat a little nearer, to show her the note that he had carried in his bosom——I have told it! And——but I must not proceed. A love-scene, ever so beautiful in itself, will not bear telling. And so I shall leave a little gap just here, which you may fill up as you please. . . . Somehow, they never knew how, they got to talking about the future instead of the past, after that, and to planning their two lives as one life. And . . . And when Miss Nancy and Mrs. Thomson returned later in the evening, Ralph was standing by the mantelpiece, but Shocky noticed that his chair was close to Hannah's. And good Miss Nancy Sawyer looked in Hannah's face and was happy.

CHAPTER XXXIV

"HOW IT CAME OUT"

WE are all children in reading stories. We want more than all else to know how it all came out at the end, and, if our taste is not perverted, we like it to come out well. For my part, ever since I began to write this story, I have been anxious to know how it was going to come out.

Well, there were very few invited. It took place at ten in the morning. The "preacher-in-charge" came, of course. Miss Nancy Sawyer was there. But Ralph's uncle was away, and Aunt Matilda had a sore throat and couldn't come. Perhaps the memory of the fact that she had refused Mrs. Thomson, the pauper, a bed for two nights, affected her throat. But Miss Nancy and her sister were there, and the preacher. And that was all, besides the family, and Bud and Martha. Of course Bud and Martha came. And driving Martha to a wedding in a "jumper" was the one opportunity Bud needed. His hands were busy, his big boots were out of sight, and it was so easy to slip from Ralph's love affair to his own, that Bud somehow, in pulling Martha Hawkins's shawl about her, stammered out half a proposal, which Martha, generous soul, took for the whole ceremony, and accepted. And Bud was so happy that Ralph guessed from his face and voice that the agony was over, and Bud was betrothed at last to the "gal as was a gal."

And after Ralph and Hannah were married— there was no trip, Ralph only changed his boarding-place and became head of the house at Mrs. Thom-son's thereafter—after it was all over, Bud came to Mr. Hartsook, and, snickering just a little, said as how as him and Martha had fixed it all up, and now they wanted to ax his advice; and Martha, proud but blushing, came up and nodded assent. Bud said as how as he hadn't got no book-larnin' nor nothin', and as how as he wanted to be somethin', and put in his best licks fer Him, you know. And that Marthy, she was of the same way of thinkin', and that was a blessin'. And the Squire was a-goin' to marry agin', and Marthy would ruther vacate. And his mother and Mirandy was sech as he wouldn't take no wife to. And he thought as how Mr. Hartsook might think of some way or some place where he and Marthy mout make a livin' fer the present, and put in their best licks fer Him, you know.

Ralph thought a moment. He was about to make an allusion to Hercules and the Augean stables, but he remembered that Bud would not understand it, though it might remind Martha of something she had seen at the East, the time she was to Bosting.

"Bud, my dear friend," said Ralph, "it looks a little hard to ask you to take a new wife"—here Bud looked admiringly at Martha—"to the poor-house. But I don't know anywhere where you can do so much good for Christ as by taking charge of that place, and I can get the appointment for you. The new commissioners want just such a man."

"What d'ye say, Marthy?" said Bud.

"Why, somebody ought to do for the poor, and I should like to do it."

And so Hercules cleaned the Augean stables.

And so my humble, homely Hoosier story of twenty years ago[1] draws to a close, and not without regret I take leave of Ralph and Hannah; and Shocky, and Bud, and Martha, and Miss Nancy, and of my readers.

P. S.—A copy of the Lewisburg *Jeffersonian* came into my hands to-day, and I see by its columns that Ralph Hartsook is principal of the Lewisburg Academy. It took me some time, however, to make out that the sheriff of the county, Mr. Israel W. Means, was none other than my old friend Bud, of the Church of the Best Licks. I was almost as much puzzled over his name as I was when I saw an article in a city paper, by Prof. W. J. Thomson, on Poor-Houses. I should not have recognized the writer as Shocky, had I not known that Shocky has given his spare time to making outcasts feel that God has not forgot.

---

[1] Written in 1871.

The MODERN READERS'
SERIES

The MODERN READERS' SERIES

Ashley H. Thorndike, *General Editor*

THE MODERN READERS' SERIES presents the world's best literature of every type: famous novels, and newer fiction of permanent interest; poetry; noted essays and dramas; eminent works of history, economics, science, philosophy, and education. American literature is given a prominent place. Unusual and hitherto inaccessible books will be found among the titles as will also translations of foreign books that have become a traditional part of a literary background.

In general, the titles in the series are available in two bindings: the one, a rich, dark green, half leather; the other, a handsome, durable blue cloth.

Volumes Published

IN HALF LEATHER
AND IN BLUE CLOTH

(All of these titles are unabridged)

AESOP: *The Fables of*. Edited by Jacobs. (In leather only.)
ALCOTT: *Little Women*
ALLEN: *A Kentucky Cardinal and Aftermath*
ARNOLD: *Culture and Anarchy*
BORROW: *Lavengro*
BRONTË: *Jane Eyre*
BROWN: *Edgar Huntly*
*BROWNING: *Selected Poems*
BURNS: *Selected Poems*
*BUTLER: *The Way of All Flesh*
BYRON: *Don Juan*

CARLYLE: *Past and Present Sartor Resartus*
COLERIDGE: *Biographia Literaria*
CONGREVE: *The Comedies of*
COOPER: *The Last of the Mohicans; The Spy*
DANA: *Two Years before the Mast*
DARWIN: *The Origin of Species*
DICKENS: *A Tale of Two Cities*

* Cannot be sold in British Dominions

61528

The MODERN READERS' SERIES

(*Continued from previous page*)

*DOSTOEVSKY: *Crime and Punishment*
*ELIOT: *Middlemarch*
EMERSON: *Essays*
FRANKLIN: *The Autobiography of Benjamin Franklin*
GOLDSMITH: *The Vicar of Wakefield*
HARTE: *The Luck of Roaring Camp and Selected Stories and Poems*
HAWTHORNE: *The Scarlet Letter*
HAZLITT: *Essays*
*IBSEN: *Plays*
*JAMES: *Daisy Miller*
KEATS: *Complete Poems*
LAMB: *The Essays of Elia*
*LONDON: *The Call of the Wild and Other Stories*
MACAULAY: *Historical Essays*
*MEREDITH: *The Ordeal of Richard Feverel*

MILL: *On Liberty and Other Essays*
MILTON: *Areopagitica and Other Prose Writings*
NEIHARDT: *The Song of Three Friends and the Song of Hugh Glass*
*PATER: *Marius the Epicurean*
POLO: *The Book of Ser Marco Polo ("Travels")*
SHERIDAN: *Plays*
*STEVENSON: *Treasure Island*
STOWE: *Uncle Tom's Cabin*
SWIFT: *Gulliver's Travels*
*TENNYSON: *Idylls of the King*
THACKERAY: *Henry Esmond*
TROLLOPE: *Barchester Towers*
TWAIN: *The Innocents Abroad*
WHITE: *A Certain Rich Man*
WILKINSON: *Contemporary Poetry*
WORDSWORTH: *Poems*

IN BLUE CLOTH ONLY

(Abridged titles are indicated)

BARKER: *Forty-Minute Plays from Shakespeare* (Abr.)
BLACKMORE: *Lorna Doone* (Abr.)
CERVANTES: *Don Quixote* (Abr.)
COOPER: *The Pathfinder* (Abr.)
DICKENS: *David Copperfield* (Abr.)
DUMAS: *The Three Musketeers* (Abr.)
*GARLAND: *A Son of the Middle Border*

HOMER: *The Iliad* (Abr.)
PORTER: *The Scottish Chiefs* (Abr.)
RIIS: *The Making of an American*
SCOTT: *The Heart of Midlothian* (Abr.)
Ivanhoe (Abr.)
SMITH: *Short Plays by Representative Authors*
THACKERAY: *Vanity Fair* (Abr.)
WATTS: *Nathan Burke*
WISTER: *Lady Baltimore*

For further details, including titles in preparation, write for complete circular.

---

* Cannot be sold in British Dominions

61528